Tapeworm

For Marianna Hofer—
Thanks for reading — hope you
enjoy

Tapeworm

Stories
by

Nicholas B. Morris

7/1/10
Denver

Monkey Puzzle Press
Boulder, Colorado

Cover Photo by Nate Jordon

Cover Design by Michael D. Edwards

Book Design by Nate Jordon

ISBN-10: 0-9826646-3-X
ISBN-13: 978-0-9826646-3-6

Monkey Puzzle Press
PO Box 20804
Boulder, CO   80308
monkeypuzzlepress.com

For Alyssa

Contents

Jawbone

WHEN I WENT TO get in his truck, there was a jawbone on the seat. I asked him what it was from. He snatched it up, dropped it behind the seat. "A deer," he said. Started the truck, told me to get in, and we left.

He turned on the radio, some country station. He didn't talk, only answered yes and no when I asked him something. Now that I knew he had a jawbone behind his seat, I was unsettled. More unsettled than I had been when I'd first seen it. Had the jawbone been long enough to belong to a deer? Could it have been a dog's? A man's?

We got to his ranch and he asked me to open the gap. I asked him what he meant and he told me to take the post out from its wire loop. I did as he said, stood in the drizzle and watched his taillights slide past. I closed the gate and got back in the truck. "Cow's over there." He pointed toward the far side of the pasture, started driving in that direction.

He got out of his truck, and while he loaded his rifle he told me about the time his daddy stepped on a landmine. The cow was bawling, her front leg at an angle nature never intended. The air was thick with her cries of pain. He shot the cow without flinching, carried on with his story in the sudden ringing silence. I wasn't really listening. I was still thinking about my friend, whom I'd last seen years ago in a city hundreds of miles from here, and the jawbone I'd seen in his truck. Hadn't there been canines? Do deer even have canines? He hadn't had any qualms about blasting the cow. Did he shoot everything as easily?

"Come on," he called to me from beside the dead cow, his knife appearing from nowhere. "You gonna help me, or let good meat go to waste?"

Custy's Used Auto

for Caleb Hicks

HIGHWAY 79 LEADING TO Caddo Peak looked the same as it always had—towns with one gas station and four churches, pine trees as far as the eye could see, deer crossing and brakes screeching. And then Prince Hill, a steep drive down from the Ouachita Mountains and into the valley where Hernando De Soto recorded facing the fiercest Indians he'd ever seen—"fought like demons" was the phrase on the historical marker overlooking the town.

John had often felt fierce in the Peak, and hadn't been back since his mother's funeral seven years earlier. If there had been a closer relative to bury his father, he would have never returned.

There was a sheriff's cruiser waiting when he pulled into his father's driveway. The sheriff stepped out of his father's house, shielded his eyes and grinned.

"John D. Custy! How the hell you been?"

John shut the car door. His father's dog bolted past the sheriff and started barking at his car.

"I've been better." He kicked at the dog, but the mutt jumped back, growling at him. "Can't you just put this one down or somethin?"

"Your daddy loved that dawg. Be a shame to kill him."

John stuck out his hand. "Good to see you, Brad."

Brad pulled John into an embrace. "Been a long time, bud."

"Sure has. They done made you sheriff?"

"Elected me last November, when Evans retired." He shifted his weight, shoulders lowering from his normal on-duty stance. "How you takin it, John? You doin okay?"

"I'm fine, Brad. Cancer gives a hell of a warnin, and we were never that close anyway. Shouldn't you be out makin a bust or kissin a baby somewhere?"

Brad handed him a card. "My home number's on the back. Call me if you need me." He climbed into his cruiser and backed out of the driveway. "Good to have you back in the Peak."

The dog was barking at John. He threw a rock at it and missed.

"Why don't you just run off to the cemetery and get a head start on the old man's grave?"

Almost 3,000 people lived in Caddo Peak, and John guessed most of them were at his father's funeral. They passed on their respects, regards, regrets, and condolences. They asked if he was making it okay. They asked if he was going to stay in town for long. They told him stories about his father selling them their car, the very one they drove to the church today. Faces he barely remembered. Seven years or more since he'd seen any of them. He hoped it would be even longer before he saw them again.

The day after the burial, John went to see his father's lawyer.

"David was a good man," the lawyer said. "Pillar of this community. The Peak won't be the same without him."

"I'm sure it won't," John said.

"So I figure this ain't no social call. You want to know what the old man left."

John didn't say anything.

"Well, the house of course. And the property it's on." The lawyer leaned back in his overstuffed chair, tugging on his red suspenders.

"You in the market for a dog?" John asked.

"Got three already."

"So that's it? House, an acre of land, and a mutt?"

"Well, the car dealership's yours too, of course. And the cars on the lot, naturally."

"So no money? No bank accounts?"

"What was left covered his funeral expenses and after my

fees, everything's supposed to go to Living Rock Methodist."

John blew out a long breath.

"Course, the way I see it," the lawyer continued, "you could make a pretty penny sellin his place and the dealership."

John and the lawyer talked for a little while longer and the lawyer agreed to buy the house and the property, but had no interest in the lot or the cars. As part of the deal, John would live in the house rent free until he could sell the dealership.

Geneva Trout, his father's loyal secretary, had been in the office since 7:30 AM. The coffee was already cold when he arrived.

"Anybody stop by to look?"

She looked up from whatever she was typing. "Look for what, Mr. Custy?"

"At. Has anyone looked *at* the cars?"

"No, Mr. Custy." Back to her typing.

"You know, I plan on sellin this place."

She paused only long enough to push the typewriter carriage back.

"I assume whoever buys it will keep you on. Did David provide you with a retirement of any kind?"

The bell on the front door jingled.

"You'd better go see what they want, Mr. Custy."

For lunch, John went to the Lux Café, a greasy-spoon diner off Highway 79. He sat on one of the green vinyl barstools at the counter.

Michelle Crenshaw, who'd been in the grade above him in high school, brought him a menu and a glass of water.

"Howya been, John?"

"Pretty good, I guess. Know anyone who wants to buy a car lot?"

Michelle shrugged. "Nobody in the Peak could afford it even if they wanted it. The guy down at the other end of the counter ain't from around here. He might be interested."

John turned and looked at the man. "Say, mister, you wouldn't be interested in buyin a used car dealership, would you?"

"No thanks," he said. "I'm just passing through."

"Yeah, I'm tryin to just pass through myself. I kind of got stuck with the place."

"How do you get stuck with a car dealership?"

He introduced himself to the man, whose name was Ed Wheeler. After explaining his situation, he asked where Wheeler was headed, what business he was in, if he wanted to buy a car here so he could avoid state taxes. Wheeler asked John about growing up in Caddo Peak, what the dotcom boom had been like, what he planned on doing with his car lot. They shook hands as they were leaving, and John waved to Wheeler as he pulled his gray Tahoe onto the highway.

His lunch seemed like a long forgotten dream by nightfall.

John held a flashlight about two feet long. He tried to turn it on, but nothing happened. He opened the back and saw the flashlight's chamber was empty.

His father was standing next to him. "John, the batteries."

David pulled the batteries for the flashlight from his ear, each making a buzzing sound as he removed them.

Sunlight poured through his window. He shut off his alarm clock and got dressed to go to the car lot.

When he arrived at Custy's Used Auto, a gray 2004 Tahoe was sitting on the lot. The door was unlocked and the keys sat in the passenger's seat.

John questioned Geneva about the Tahoe, but she only shrugged. "Your father handled the cars. I just take care of the books. Probably some old distributor didn't realize he died and shipped an old order." She didn't have any ideas about the lack of an invoice.

That afternoon, someone came in and asked about the Tahoe.

"I just got it on the lot today, so I don't really have a price yet. Give me about twenty minutes and I'll get back to you."

John looked up the Blue Book value of the Tahoe and added fifteen percent.

After the man signed the paperwork, John treated him to a chicken-fried steak at the Lux.

His father's mutt was barking at the door. John let him out and saw Brad Partain pulling in the driveway.

"What's the trouble?" John asked.

"Did you talk to a fella from out of town yesterdy? At the Lux?"

"Yeah. Umm . . . Wheeler. Ed Wheeler."

"He say where he was goin?"

"I don't really remember. Why?"

"One of my deputies found a body down toward Lake Clarence. Turns out to be the fella you had lunch with. Mind if I ask you some questions?"

"Go ahead."

"Do you know what he was drivin?"

"A gray Tahoe. I sold one just like it this afternoon."

The sheriff's eyes lit up. "You sure it wasn't the same one?"

"Not really."

"Who'd you sell it to?"

"Some guy. I didn't know him, but he really wanted to buy it."

"You got records on the guy?"

"Back at the office."

Brad spit, a brown sliver of tobacco rolled down his chin,

and he nodded toward his car. "Feel like takin a ride?"

The local paper carried the story of a Caddo County resident, a pig farmer, who was arrested for the brutal murder of a businessman passing through the area.

John got a thrill seeing himself quoted in all the articles, pinning Wendell Jackson, the man who had bought the Tahoe, to the crime. Sheriff Partain and the county prosecutor believed Jackson had parked the Tahoe at Custy's Used Auto, then returned that afternoon to "buy it" before the body was discovered and the Tahoe seized as evidence.

A few days before he was to appear before the grand jury, John drove up on the lot to discover another new vehicle, this one a Jeep. Again, the keys lay on the passenger's seat. He called Brad Partain immediately.

"So it was just sittin here, like the Tahoe." Partain rubbed the brown slime on his chin.

"Same setup. Same spot even."

Partain looked at Geneva. "You didn't see nothin?"

"I just keep the books, Sheriff. I don't pay any attention to the lot."

Partain shrugged. "Well, I'll tell the boys to keep an eye out. If somebody shows up wantin to buy it real quick, be sure and let me know."

The temperature dropped when the sun went down, but the humidity hung in the air like a wet blanket. John barely moved as he sat under the fans—his father hadn't believed in paying for air conditioning. He tossed and turned, kicked off the sheets and lay directly under the fan, trying to fall asleep.

The dog started barking somewhere near the woodline.

"Shut up!"

The barking got louder. The dog started to growl.

"Shut the fuck up!" John covered his head with the pillow.

The dog kept barking.

He got out of bed, stomped to the front door, turned on the light and stepped onto the porch. "Hey, mutt! If you don't quiet down, you're gonna get a permanent worm treatment!"

The dog finally stopped barking and trotted back to the porch.

John got back in bed and tried to sleep, but instead stared out the window and watched the sky grow lighter.

"You look rough. Are you feelin okay?" Geneva asked the instant he walked in the door.

"Damn dog kept me up all night."

"Sheriff Partain called. Said to remind you about your testimony this afternoon."

"Shit. Take care of the office, I've got to go home and change."

"But I only . . ."

"Then take the day off." He slammed the door behind him.

When he got home, he quickly put on his suit, looked at himself in the mirror. His eyes were bloodshot from lack of sleep, and no matter how many times he ran a brush through his hair it looked like he'd just woke up.

He fixed himself a sandwich and ate it in his father's recliner, looking up at the clock every few minutes. The sandwich was resting half-eaten on his stomach when the phone rang.

"Hello?"

"Where're you at?" It was Brad Partain.

"I'm at home. Must've dozed off."

"Well get down here. You've got to testify if we're gonna make a case on this guy."

"I'll be there as soon as I can."

The judge called John to the stand.

A lawyer approached him. "Mr. Custy, are you aware that the accused blew a goldfish through the mail slot of the senior senator from Idaho?"

"Excuse me?"

"Answer the question please," the judge said from under his orange tophat.

"I was not aware." He looked around the room for Partain, but couldn't find him. "Am I done here, Your Honor?"

"You are excused."

When he opened the door of the courtroom, the hallway was dark and musty. He walked toward the nearest opening.

"John! Over here!"

Wheeler was calling to him from the bathroom door.

"I need to talk to you, John."

Where the urinals would normally be was the lunch counter they'd ate at the day they met, complete with Michelle Crenshaw.

"Pull out your hair and help me weave a blanket," Wheeler said to him when Michelle set down their food. "I need to fight off the flu like a bullfighter."

John looked down at his plate. There was a cellphone surrounded by parsley. It started to ring but when he tried to pick it up it fell to the floor and shattered into slivers of glass.

He stood, looked into the mirror, and saw the woodline beside his father's house. Two red beams of light burned out of the dark and moved closer. Blackness began to fill the room like smoke.

Outside, his father's dog was barking and snarling. John looked at the red digits of his alarm clock—4:13 AM. He got out of bed, went in the living room, turned on the TV. He had to know that he was back in the real world again.

When he got to the lot, there was a new truck sitting next to the Jeep.

Geneva was bouncing in her seat when he walked in. "Have you heard?"

"Heard what?"

"They let that Wendell Jackson feller go. Said the evidence wasn't strong enough to keep him."

"Did you see anybody out here this mornin? Puttin that new truck on the lot?"

She shook her head. "Do you still plan on sellin this place, Mr. Custy? I need to know if I should be lookin for another job."

"As soon as I find someone to buy it." He walked into his office and shut the door.

A few minutes later, she knocked on his door. "Mr. Custy? A man's come to see you about buyin a truck for his son. He really likes the new one."

Partain's cruiser pulled up to his porch, the dog barking in the driveway.

"Howya doin, John?"

"Pretty good, Brad. Yourself?"

Partain took a deep breath, exhaled. "I've had better days."

"What's on your mind?"

"One of my deputies found another body down seventy-nine. Might be the guy that owned that Jeep somebody left on your lot."

"What happened with Jackson?"

"Well, this, among other things. What was wrong with you in court?"

"I haven't been sleepin well. When I do sleep, I have very strange dreams."

Partain spit and rubbed his chin.

"Am I a suspect, Brad?"

"We don't have any suspects at the moment," Partain said, "but I'd keep my nose clean if I was you."

John sat in his recliner, trying to find something interesting enough on TV to keep him awake. He didn't care if he had another dream for years.

He stopped on *Law and Order*. They usually got the right suspect in the end. John thought about being a suspect, and suddenly wasn't in the mood for *Law and Order*.

Local news. Report about the man killed off of Highway 79. John watched for half a minute before he changed the station.

Cops. Next.

Sitcom. Sitcom. Church channel. Sitcom. Twenty-four hour news channel. 70s sitcom. An old black-and-white movie. John stopped. Charlie Chaplin in *The Great Dictator*. A good laugh would keep him up.

Charlie Chaplin removed his mask to reveal his true identity: Brad Partain. He stepped out of the TV into the living room. "If you fart on the geese," he said, "you must also juggle the overhead fan or the alarm will go off."

Geneva Trout's head peeked in from the kitchen. "Someone on the phone for you, Mr. Custy."

John snapped awake. *The Great Dictator* had given way to *The Manchurian Candidate*. He walked into the kitchen to brew a pot of coffee.

He went to the car lot the next morning with heavy eyes and his stomach in knots from the coffee he'd drunk all night. Geneva said something to him when he walked in, but he didn't really hear it.

"I'll be in my office," he mumbled, shutting the door behind him.

John looked up the numbers of other car dealers in the

region to see if they would be interested in taking over Custy's Used Auto. He was ready to get back to the semi-retired life of an ex-dotcommer working at his computer, rather than sitting in a musty office building in Nowheresville, Arkansas, trying to sell used cars. But his eyes would barely stay open, so he laid his head down on his desk to rest them.

When he awoke, it was dark outside. He wondered how he could have slept all day.

He stood and stretched, stiff from sleeping at his desk. He opened the door to his office and walked into the front part of the building. There was a commotion outside.

When he opened the door, he saw no one, but there was a Chevy Impala on the lot where there hadn't been before.

John ran out, looking in all directions. He scanned the dark, but could find nothing. He turned to go back inside, but caught a movement in his peripheral vision. He turned to see what it was and his vision filled with blackness.

He awoke again somewhere in the woods, but there was a dirt road beneath him and a car nearby. He looked down at himself and saw he was covered in blood.

John quickly checked himself to see if he was injured, but nothing seemed to be wrong. All he found was a set of keys in his hand. He tried to stand, but tripped and fell over something. It was a human body, mutilated beyond recognition.

John turned and vomited, as much from the rancid smell as the sight. He stood and got into the car. In the distance, he could hear sirens approaching.

As the door of his cell slammed shut, Partain spit on him. The stench of his Skoal was overwhelming.

"Brad, you know I couldn't do somethin like this."

"Don't call me Brad, you sonofabitch." Partain turned on his heel and disappeared.

John sat on the bunk. He must be guilty. They had found him next to a body, covered in blood. If this was the old days, they'd probably have already hung him from the tree casting a shadow on the floor through the cell window.

The shadow shifted, moving across the wall before it disappeared altogether.

John stood on his bunk and looked through the barred window. He caught a glimpse of a creature he didn't recognize, something large and lumbering, fading into the darkness among the trees.

Plea Bargain

After Burroughs

RED AND BLUE SCREAMING out of the dark . . . bright glare from flashlight . . . "License and registration, son" . . .

The Kid can't walk a straight line, can't stand on one foot with his finger on his nose, doesn't know his ABCs backwards . . . bracelets snap over his wrists.

From the backseat of the cruiser he sees the cop smile smugly, holding a joint up in the headlights.

Booking room . . . Fingerprints . . .

"Gettin yer pitcher taken fer yer momma?" . . .

"He got anymore on him?"

Shoes, pockets, tongue, ears, and asshole poked and prodded by the Local Finest . . .

"He tellya where he got it? Who his buddies are?"

"Nah, he ain't talkin . . . where's yer buddies now?" Beady cop eyes leering over a dyed black moustache . . .

"Look, this ain't necessary. I got paid today, so I can pay my bond. Just let me out and y'all can go back to harassin the niggers."

"Oh, a wiseass . . . tell im what we do to wiseasses, Tommy."

Tommy snaps the rubber glove he's wearing. His beergut jiggles with every goofy laughing breath.

"Prob'ly a dealer if he's got money on him."

"I ain't no fuckin dealer."

"And a dirty mouth too. Tell im, Tommy. Tell im what happens to young boys with dirty mouths."

Tommy wears a stupid sly grin.

Cold cell, wet floor. The Kid's socks and shoes have been removed—"suicide watch," the turnkey said. The Kid wonders who ever killed themselves over one joint.

"Why'm I still in here?" he yells to the passing guard. "My money not good enough for you?"

"Shut up or we'll blast you with the hose again."

Thinks about his friends who left the party before and after him . . . wonders what happened to them.

"Hey, Kid, you got a visitor."

The man on the other side of the bars wears a military uniform, medals gleaming on his chest from the overhead light.

"I'd like to talk to you for a minute, son. Go ahead, Chuck, open the door—he ain't gonna hurt me."

"Sure thing, Captain."

The man in uniform enters and sticks out his hand. "I'm Captain Bucky Beachhead."

The Kid folds his arms over his chest.

"You want I should mace im?" the guard says from behind.

"That'll be all, thanks, Chuck." He turns back to the Kid. "That's some wiseass yer sittin on. You can keep sittin on it in here and places like it, or you can listen to me and get outta here."

"I'm listenin."

Beachhead looks down at the file in his hand. "So here's what yer lookin at, Kid—a high school dropout with no steady job and a drug bust on yer record . . . or . . ."

"Or what?"

"Or you sign up with the Army, and we make sure the charges get lost behind a filin cabinet somewhere. And you're a hero to your family and community, of course."

"What's the catch?"

"Free schoolin, free housin, free medical and dental, good job referrals when you get out, and you don't go to jail."

"What about the war?"

Beachhead's gaze piercing, level, boring through to the back of his skull. The Kid feels like he's got a sniper's dot tattooed on his forehead.

"So what's it gonna be . . . the bum that everyone uses as an example for their kids *not* to be, or the admiration of everyone you know?"

"And the possession charge goes bye-bye?"

"Any minute a strong wind's gonna carry it away . . . so long as I lift the paperweight."

A piece of paper with a dotted line at the bottom appears seemingly from nowhere.

"Room for one more inside, son."

The Big Wheel

AUGUST WAS THE WORST month to be a carnie in the South. Working twelve-hour shifts in humid hellholes like Alabama was no way to live, even in the best of years. And this had not been the best of years for Ernest Sutton. He felt a sudden nostalgia for the 90s, when he'd been a roadie for Billy Ray Cyrus, and lit a cigarette.

"Step right up, girls n boys," he said, an unenthusiastic version of his carnie routine. "Take a spin on the big wheel."

Ernest was running the Ferris wheel this week, and possibly for the rest of the season. He usually ran booth games, shucking singles off rubes brave and dumb enough to toss rings, throw softballs at bottles, or lob footballs at toilet lids in the hope of winning cheap prizes. But he'd pissed off Peter Trammell, the fair's manager, handing over a light cashbag once too often. Trammell accused him of skimming. Ernest skimmed, sure—"You wouldn't trust me if I didn't steal a little, right?"

Trammell was not amused, so he was on Ferris wheel duty until further notice.

While the hayseeds spun in vertical circles, he wondered where he would make the money to pay off Trammell. In the past, he'd slung weed, meth, and occasionally coke on the side, but all his connections had been busted over the years and since he was never anywhere more than a week, he couldn't make new ones. Any drugs he bought now came from kids selling at the fair.

Pull the lever, open the gates, new round of rubes on the big wheel. Instead of taking dollars, he tore little red tickets and stuffed them in a wooden box.

Halfway through the night, Trammell stopped by the Ferris wheel.

"Things runnin smooth over here?"

"Around and around and around." Ernest lit another Marlboro.

"Good. Prove to me you can't fuck up a trained-monkey gig, maybe you can go back to booths."

"Course it never hurts none to grease the wheels, huh? Zat what you're sayin?"

"Take it however you want. But you know good as anybody that money talks and bullshit spins a goddamn Ferris wheel the whole summer."

Ernest flicked his cigarette and yanked the lever, bringing the wheel to a sudden stop. "Shouldn't you be over at the pie-eatin contest? Or did they cancel it?"

"You so funny, how come you a carnie stead of a comedian?" Trammell laughed at his own joke and waddled into the neon-lit night.

Ernest woke up in the same green, white, and rust 1971 Winnebago he'd started the circuit in twelve years before. The walls were cracked, thin and papery, wet from various sources over the years: roof leaks, spilled beer, crude sexual malfunctions. Occasionally a cockroach would crawl across the wall, scuttling from one corner to another. *Either everywhere in a four state radius has the same kind of roach,* he thought, *or the fuckin things have stowed away in my house.*

He shoved a pizza box full of cigarette butts onto the floor. It skittered across the Keystone cans covering the sticky linoleum. His air conditioner wheezed and sputtered; every few minutes a drop slid off and fell to the floor.

I got to start makin some money today.

He got his first break when one of the kids separated from his parents a few yards away.

"I wanna ride the big wheel, Daddy."

"Got your tickets?"

"Uh-huh."

The man handed his son a ten. "I'm takin yer sister to the bumper cars. When yer done, go git you a snack and sit down over there."

"Okay."

Ernest cracked his knuckles. *Showtime.*

The boy started up the boarding ramp.

"Hey, kid." Ernest leaned in conspiratorially as he took the ticket. "You wanna take a ride on the special seat?"

"Special seat?"

"Yeah, the super spinny one. You can ride it for ten, but you gotta be careful—might spin over and dump you out."

The kid's eyes shown so bright Ernest could see his reflection. The bill appeared like a magic trick.

"Step over here," Ernest said. "I'll let you know which one it is."

At the end of the day, he only made thirty bucks off the spinny seat gimmick; most kids didn't care enough to part with their allowance money. He could only afford a new carton of smokes.

The next day, he decided on grossout bets.

Two junior high kids wandered past the wheel, smoking thin cigarettes as they gawked at the girls' denim-clad asses ahead of them.

"Scuse me fellas, what ya smokin?"

The teenagers looked busted. "All we could get was my mom's Virginia Slims," the taller one said.

"I bet you twenty I can smoke a Slim in one drag."

"And if you don't?"

Ernest produced his crumpled box of reds. "I'll give you the rest of this pack and buy you a new one."

"Deal." One of them pulled out a Slim, snickering at the prospect of real cigarettes.

Ernest hawked a lugey, spit, lit the cigarette. He took a long slow drag, watching the orange ember burn all the way to the filter.

He exhaled in the boys' faces.

"Twenty bucks."

They handed him two tens and walked away cursing.

He did similar stunts throughout the day—eating crickets, putting cigarettes out on his tongue, even picking gum off the underside of a seat and chewing it. By the end of his shift, he'd made almost $200.

But when he got back to the Winnebago, he found someone had slashed his tires. He pictured an angry boyfriend with a pocketknife and a crying girlfriend. He bought a set of used tires, then only had enough money left for a bottle of bourbon and a cheeseburger from the local drive-through.

He'd watched the big wheel turning for ten days, and Ernest still didn't know how or where he could make a little extra cash. He thought about gambling with some of the other carnies, but knew he'd get swindled, especially if they figured out why he was suddenly so keen to bet with them. He thought about finding a blood or sperm bank, but realized nobody would want anything to do with his fluids after he'd picked up hepatitis in a tattoo parlor. Occasionally, he even fantasized about prostituting himself to the rich girls who passed him for a seat on the Ferris wheel. But he realized that a girl with money wouldn't even glance at a graying longhair with obscene tattoos covering his sleeveless arms. *I'd have a better shot at tryin to bed an old lady*, he thought. *Besides, even an old broad who needed it pretty bad would run if she saw the 'bago.*

"Got any good schemes yet?"

Trammell had walked up behind him as he was staring into space.

"Be a hell of a lot easier to slip you some extra money if I was runnin somethin that took dollars instead of tickets."

"Resourceful man like you?" Trammell's grin was large and toothy. "Shit, I'm surprised you still runnin the wheel. You ain't got no insurance you can cash in?"

Ernest lit a cigarette off a red ticket. "Why the fuck would I need insurance?"

Trammell laughed. "Well, I can see you deep in thought. Night, Ernie."

Ernest flipped him off. "Sleep tight, Precious."

She was in line for the fourth time, her eyes boring into him again. He winked as she passed.

She wasn't normally his type: a big shy farm girl who'd probably never seen a man outside her family, church, or school in her entire life. Any other time, he'd have looked right through her, or conned her into a blowjob behind a booth. But with the losing streak he'd been on, his standards were low and if he had a chance at prostitution, she was it.

He left her up a long time, building his courage. *If I do this right, I'll be back in the booths next week.* He took a deep breath, stopped the wheel, and waited for her to come down the ramp.

One "Hey there, pretty lady" later and they were sharing grape snowcones. Her name was Amanda; she'd come to the fair with her boyfriend, who she'd caught flirting with some cowgirl. She'd stormed off, saw Ernest and was smitten. Her daddy ran a cattle farm and her momma directed the choir at church. She wanted to see bright lights, big cities, and as much dick as she could get her hands on.

When she paid for the snowcones, Ernest saw her wallet was stuffed with tens and twenties.

He was steering her back toward the lot where the 'bago was parked, with promises of bourbon and a sweaty good time, and would have made it if his path wasn't blocked by Trammell.

"Ain't you sposed to be workin the wheel, Ernie?"

"Just takin a quick break. Back in twenty minutes or so."

"Who's yo friend?"

Amanda's eyes dug into the ground, her talkative voice suddenly silent.

Before anyone else could speak, Trammell continued.

"I knew Ernie here was good yankin a handle," he said, waving his hand back and forth. "I didn't know he was into judgin heifers too."

Amanda tore away from Ernest's arm, jogged sobbing into the neon night.

"That fat girl was gonna give me your money," he said.

Trammell was laughing hard. "That fat girl was gonna move you into a trailer park. I just saved yo life."

Ernest went back to the wheel and hoped Amanda would return. He needed to get laid at least as bad as he needed money.

After the fair shut down at midnight, Ernest lay awake, sweating in spite of the air conditioner that rattled and coughed all night. His money situation didn't make it any easier to sleep, and he was becoming familiar with the rising light of dawn. But as he lit his first smoke of the day, he got an idea.

He found a wifebeater that passed the smell test, already feeling better about the day. He'd be able to go back to life behind a booth instead of staring at the bottoms of shoes all day. He might even gain a little respect from Trammell, if there was any respect in the man.

He pounded on Trammell's trailer door. Trammell opened it wearing only boxers.

"Goddamn, you too ugly to be the first thing I see in the mornin. Fuck you want?"

"I know how you can get your money back."

Trammell snickered. "Why do I got to get it back? You the one lost it."

"You ain't even gonna listen?"

Trammell shifted his weight from one leg to the other. The trailer groaned on its wheels.

"We fight for it."

Trammell cracked up. His belly and mantits jiggled as the trailer creaked. "That's the funniest shit I ever heard. This ain't about the fat girl, is it?"

"Fuck you. Look, tonight we fight in the big pavilion out front and charge admission. That way, you get your money back and I get to go back to the booths."

"You sound awful sure you gonna win."

"You ain't never fought a little guy before? We'll kick your ass. Besides, we're in Klan country. These cornfeds ain't gonna stand for a white man gettin his ass kicked by some big coon." He hoped the race baiting would work if nothing else did.

"You think I'm scared of them? Probly gonna be at least as many brothas out there as Klan." He snorted. "You gonna get the beatin of yo life tonight, cracker, and ain't no white brotherhood gonna save you from that. You better get Jesus on yo side. Least he knew how to take a whuppin."

"So we're on then."

"Not so fast. You say if you win, you go back to the booths. But what if you lose? What do I get?" He paused. "I tell you what—when I win, you fired."

Ernest stared at him, the grin on Trammell's face growing wider.

"Deal," he said.

"See yo ass at eight o'clock then."

Ernest spent the afternoon doing pushups, situps, and flexing in his hazy mirror. He thought he was in pretty good shape for a man pushing forty, except for the knife scar on his chest.

At 7:30 PM, he left his trailer and headed for the pavilion. On the way, he passed a flier he didn't recognize:

TONIGHT
Bareknuckle Boxing Match
Ernie "Ferris Wheel" Sutton
vs.
Peter "The Beater" Trammell
8:00 @ Pike County Fairgrounds Pavilion
Admission $5

Trammell had gone all out for the fight. There was a mat set up, complete with ropes. There was even a bell in one corner.

At 7:55 PM, Trammell waded through the crowd, stepped through the ropes. He was wearing basketball shorts that clung to his massive thighs and a t-shirt that said *Your Mama Screams My Name In Bed*. Sweat streamed down his face, but his grin was as wide as ever.

"Ready to get your ass kicked by a scrawny white boy?" Ernest said.

"Talk shit while you still got teeth, Ernie. Ya see the flier? Like the nickname?"

"Thought it was cute. Not as cute as 'The Peter Beater' or whatever you called yourself, but cute."

The girl who ran the knife-throwing booth stepped into the ring and made the announcements. The crowd roared as the bell rang and they stepped toward each other, fists raised.

Ernest felt the first blow knock his head back, the second one in his gut. *How'd he hit me so quick?* Then another to the nose. He looked up at Trammell from the ground.

"What's wrong, Ernie? Too fast?" He turned around and played to the crowd.

Ernest jumped up and rushed Trammell, who tried to move but not quickly enough. Ernest knocked him off balance, punched him once in the jaw, once in the neck. Trammell staggered, wheezing, but never fell. He stepped in to capitalize on his advantage, but didn't see Trammell's fist coming. Blood welled up in his mouth. He spit a tooth onto the concrete.

"Now you always gonna look like a carnie," Trammell laughed. "Even when you ain't one no mo."

Ernest tried to hold his ground, thinking he could tire Trammell, but the big man was quick on his feet, fists hard and sudden. Ernest managed to split one of Trammell's lips and crack his nose, but soon found himself on all fours, spitting blood and gasping for air.

Trammell laughed loud enough to be heard over the crowd. He motioned for the microphone.

"Hey, Ernie," he blasted over the speakers, "you fired!"

Then he dropped the mic, ran at Ernest, kicked him hard in the ribs. The crowd went wild.

"Off the lot by midnight, or I call the cops to impound that tetanus-infested hoopty."

When he finally made it to the Winnebago, the engine wouldn't turn over; the air conditioner had drained the battery. He thought about trying to steal a new one from one of the local yokels, but didn't have the energy.

Ernest lit his last cigarette, looked at himself in the rearview mirror. His eyes were swollen, skin bruised, cut, and bleeding. He opened his mouth—three bloody gaps where teeth had been. His hair was matted with sweat, dirt, and blood.

"Fuck," was all he could think to say.

Inside Man

for Andrew Miller

IT STARTED AS A joke.

Jack and Hank were smoking a bowl in their apartment, trying to figure out how they were going to make a little extra cash. They were both moving soon, Jack to a downtown Boulder apartment with his girlfriend Amy, Hank back to his hometown of Seattle. They had been in their current apartment for almost a year, and after the numerous problems they'd had with the place (meddling neighbors, leaks above the stairwell, leaking gas, clogged toilets, showers and garbage disposals), there was no desire to renew their lease. But there was also little money to move; Hank worked overnights at the Kinko's downtown and Jack worked as a maintenance worker at a private high school in North Boulder. Between the two, they barely made enough to keep food in the refrigerator and eviction notices off the door. Coming up with the first month's rent and deposit, as well as the general costs of moving, was going to be a challenge for them both.

"Too bad your girlfriend isn't rich," Hank said, taking in a big puff of blue smoke. "You could just hit her up for some money."

"Yeah, and she could loan you a few hundred for gas to Seattle," Jack said, taking the hot glass pipe from Hank. "Hey, as long as we're fantasizing, let's go all out."

"We could try hooking up with one of the MILFs at your school. I'm sure some of those rich bitches would throw cash at some young dick."

"You and I both wish," Jack said, passing the pipe back to Hank.

"Of course there's always the old standbys. We could knock over the liquor store around the corner."

"Fuck, if we're gonna knock over some place, I'd just as soon do it somewhere we had an inside man. Like Kinko's."

Jack looked over at Hank, expecting him to laugh, but instead, found his roommate in deep concentration.

"Hey, man, hit it or quit it."

"Sorry," Hank said, quickly taking a hit and handing it back. "I think that's a great idea."

"What?"

"The register usually has about two thousand in cash in the middle of the night, and I'll be the only one working. You can just sneak in the backdoor while I'm facing the other way, stick me up, I'll hand over the cash, and you split."

"Great plan, genius. What about the cameras?"

"You can wear that ski mask you wore when you were shoveling snow for the school. And you can wear extra clothes so it disguises your build."

"What about my voice? The cops will ask you what I sound like."

"We won't have to worry about that. You'll sneak up on me, stick a gun at my head while I'm standing at the register—like I wouldn't know what you want."

"What if somebody walks in to pick up some job they need the next morning?"

"Dude, I work the overnight all the time. Between two and four, there's jack shit going on. Nobody will show up. It'll be perfect. You'll have the alibi of being home asleep. Plus, since you don't have a car, it would take you too long to walk to Kinko's, rob the place, walk back home *and* go to work in the morning. You'll be sticking me up, and you could always tie me up so that will take the heat off my ass. Fuck, dude," he took a hit off the pipe, "we'll be able to split the money and walk away. I'll be leaving anyway, so who's gonna hold me responsible at Kinko's?"

Jack wasn't sure what to think. Hank might be joking around, playing it deadpan, but he was full of details. People with details are serious. Details mean business.

"Sounds like a pretty crazy idea, man."

"Just crazy enough to work. You up for it?"

"If you think we can get away with it . . . sure, I'm in."

"We're cop's kids, man," Hank said. "If anyone can get away with it, we can."

Jack was in bed with Amy at her apartment, staring at the late night ceiling. He told her about his half-assed idea and Hank's zest to see it through.

"Are you going to do it?"

"I was thinking about it. I mean, we grew up around cops, so we know how to think like they do. We've had to expect how they'd be looking to catch us our whole lives, so I figure that gives us the upper hand on the planning end of things, and it'll help us be extra careful when we're pulling it off." Jack took a deep breath. "Here's the thing—I'm not sure how I'm supposed to be home asleep when I'm downtown robbing Kinko's."

"I'll drive you."

"Would you really?"

Amy grinned, leaned over and kissed him. "I've always wanted to be part of a heist. Now I get to drive the getaway car." She giggled. "We'll be sexy notorious outlaws, like Bonnie and Clyde."

"I don't want to be like Bonnie and Clyde," Jack said. "That story didn't end so well."

Hank was against Amy joining the heist at first. Bringing in an outside party was dangerous, especially someone who had grown up without a police presence in the home. Hank thought she might crack under pressure.

Jack already had her alibi planned. They would take their cell phones when she picked him up, call each other when they got close to Kinko's, and Amy would wait in the car with the two phones for several minutes while Jack went inside to get the money. If the police asked about it, they couldn't sleep and called each other for a little phone sex.

Hank admitted it was a pretty good alibi. "But," he asked, "is she paranoid enough to anticipate the ways cops might get us?"

"If there's one thing I can vouch on Amy's behalf," Jack said, remembering the numerous occasions he'd had to explain some otherwise harmless action or comment, "it's that she is *very* paranoid."

The day of the heist was unseasonably warm. Only a week before, there had been five inches of snow on the ground, but a Chinook wind was blowing through the mountains and the sun baked the foothills so the temperature climbed into the sixties. Jack sweated all day at work, overdressed with his thermal underwear beneath a t-shirt—the weather had predicted a high in the low forties. *If nothing else goes wrong today*, he thought, *it could be a pretty good day.*

Jack got home from work about 5:00 PM, had a smoke and a shower. He and Hank walked over to the TexMex restaurant down the block, where they met Amy for dinner to go over last minute details: the signal, what time to arrive, etc. After a few drinks and dinner, Jack and Hank headed back to their apartment and Amy headed for her apartment on the other side of Boulder, where she'd play loud music until 11:00 PM and shut out her lights so the neighbors would think she'd gone to bed.

About 9:30 PM, Hank left for work. "Remember, don't show up before two. At two, I'll go out and smoke a cigarette if everything is clear. If I haven't come out by two-thirty, abort."

"Gotcha," Jack said. He raised the pipe in a salute. "See you in a few hours."

"I don't know what you're talking about," Hank said. "I'm just going to work. See you tomorrow afternoon when *you* get home from work."

Jack played video games for an hour or so, got stoned,

masturbated out of boredom. Around 1:30 PM, there was a small knock on the apartment door.

"Are you ready?" Amy asked.

"Ready as I'll ever be."

Jack had hoped once the sun set the temperature would drop, but the air was still warm. Under the multiple layers of clothing he wore to pad his build, he was starting to sweat before he got in the car.

He dialed up her cell phone when they neared Kinko's. "Hang up in twenty minutes," he said. She nodded, turned into the Hollywood Video parking lot across from Kinko's. The clock on the dashboard read 1:48 PM.

They waited for Hank to come out and smoke a cigarette, Amy drumming her fingers on the wheel, Jack sweating from nervousness and too many clothes. Shortly after 2:00 PM, Hank stepped out behind the store, lit a cigarette, stretched while waving the cherry in small circles.

"That's my cue," Jack said. "I should be back in ten or fifteen minutes. Wish me luck."

"Luck," Amy said. She leaned over and kissed him. "I'll be here."

Jack wiped his forehead, moved across the parking lot. There was no traffic from either direction, so he crossed and crouched behind the dumpster next to the open back door.

Hank dropped his cigarette, exhaled loudly, rubbed out the butt with his sneaker. Jack slipped the Glock his father had given him out of his jacket pocket, mopped his forehead again, counted thirty Mississippi, and crept around the corner.

Jack moved low through the back door, ducked behind a counter. He heard the humming of dozens of mechanical insects, smelled the hot, freshly printed paper. Hank was at the register, fiddling around as planned. Jack crept closer and was about to stand when he heard the front doorbell ring.

Fuck! he thought. It took all his effort not to scream. From his position behind Hank, he could hear the guy's voice, pure CU fratboy:

"Dude, I dropped off a project that's due at like eight in the morning—ya got it done yet?"

Hank noticeably stiffened. "It's not done yet. Check back in a few hours."

Fratboy wasn't buying it, getting closer to the counter. "Look, asswipe, I need that project right now!"

Jack decided it was time for action. He stood and leveled the gun at Fratboy's dyed blonde hairline.

"Stay cool and nobody eats shit," he said in what he hoped was a hoarse whisper.

Fratboy's eyes went wide. "Man, I don't want no trouble, I just got homework is all."

"Gimme your wallet."

Fratboy reached into his pocket, slid his wallet onto the counter. "Fucking pissed myself, brah," he whined.

Jack brought the butt of the pistol down on Fratboy's temple and he dropped like a bag of hammers. Aware every second of the cameras on him, Jack pointed the pistol at Hank, motioned toward the cash drawer and the open duffel bag in his other hand.

"Please just don't kill me, sir, is all I ask," Hank said as he emptied the register into the bag. "I don't want anyone to get hurt, sir."

Jack waved the gun at him to shut him up. When Hank finished filling the bag with cash, Jack motioned toward the floor, mimed putting hands on his head. Hank complied as Jack removed the duct tape from his other jacket pocket, wiped his forehead, and began to wrap Hank's wrists.

Jack had been gone about ten minutes when a patrol car pulled into the parking lot of the Hollywood Video. Amy slunk down in her seat, hoping the officer didn't come over and ask her what she was doing in an empty parking lot at 2:30 AM. But the car turned around, parked for several minutes, and pulled back out again. She sighed with relief, decided sitting in an open parking lot was too conspicuous. She then crossed the road, parking on the nearest side street. When Jack started to cross, she would flash her lights at him and they'd make a quick, inconspicuous getaway. She hoped he didn't cross the street while she was moving the car. She didn't want it to look as if she'd abandoned him.

Fratboy was groaning but not yet fully conscious when Jack finished taping Hank's wrists. After he finished, Jack did a few quick loops around the ankles, picked up the bag, and began backing toward the open door in back, gun still trained on Hank. He saw Hank's eyes get large, wondered why just about the time he backed into someone. Spinning around, Jack saw a woman wearing a black and purple Kinko's shirt. They stood staring at each other for a few seconds, then the woman started screaming. Jack covered his ears, watched in horror as she rounded the corner and took off down the street. He ran after her, but tired quickly because of his heavy clothing. He wished for a second that he had actually put bullets in the gun.

Fuck it, he thought, *I'm getting out of here.*

He bolted across the street to the Hollywood Video parking lot, but found it empty. Someone across the street was flashing their headlights, but he didn't stick around long enough to see what they wanted. He could already hear sirens approaching, so he took off running, tearing off clothing to make it easier.

He turned into a narrow alley, spotted three dumpsters. He found the one for paper recycling, jumped in, and closed the top cover. Clutching the duffel bag to his chest, he tried to stop his heaving breath, realized how much pot he'd been smoking the last few years. Vaguely, he heard sirens passing on the street.

The dumpster was hot, and he was about to climb out and

look for Amy when he heard a car pull into the alley. He kept still and listened, wondering if they were checking the other dumpsters. He heard Amy softly calling his name, so he opened the dumpster, climbed out, and got in her car.

The cool air on the drive home never felt so good.

Second Coming

I

"DID I EVER TELL you about performing Elvis's autopsy?" his voice a hoarse whisper.

Aaron could see his father was dying. Years of Pall Malls had taken their toll, a habit driven by decades of performing autopsies. Judges all around the greater Memphis area once respected his father's opinion—if James Priestly said his results were accurate, it held the weight of a Constitutional amendment, until he performed Elvis's autopsy. But now he was a wisp of a man, lying in a hospital bed, waiting to die.

"About a million times," Aaron replied. It was his father's favorite story—the King of Rock n Roll wheeled into his examining room, yes-men and publicists milling about, pestering him about specifics, the lawyers who threatened him if he didn't alter some of the facts. It almost ruined his father's career, and Aaron didn't want that particular incident to be his father's legacy.

"But did I ever tell you about trying to get him into the freezer?" He erupted in a fit of coughing.

Aaron waited until his father recovered. "I don't remember that particular detail of the story."

"It was quite a struggle," his father said, closing his eyes. "Elvis was—well, he was fat, that's the only way to put it. He weighed about three-fifty, although they had me shave about a hundred pounds of that off the autopsy report. I didn't have a problem with that—hell, nobody wants to remember him looking like Jackie Gleason. They wanted that Mississippi Boy that couldn't show his hips on TV. But he was so damn big I wasn't going to be able to keep him in the freezer till the coffin arrived."

"So what did you do?" Aaron tried picturing his dad and half a dozen sycophants pushing on the recently deceased entertainer, Elvis's gut not giving, hanging over the opening of the freezer.

"I removed some of his fat."

"You gave Elvis post-mortem liposuction?"

His father nodded. "I had to get him in there. He died on the can, so he didn't smell too pleasant."

Normally, Aaron might have laughed. Tonight, he just hoped his father would be able to finish the story.

"I cut him open and vacuumed maybe a hundred, hundred-fifty pounds of pure fat out of him. Put it in medical waste containers and hid them in my basement after Elvis's entourage left."

Aaron wasn't sure if he should believe his father in this state. He had never heard his father talk about this incident before, and this stolen fat story could just be a cancerous delirium, or perhaps his father misremembering the past. Besides, he'd been down in the basement hundreds of times, and had never seen the containers.

"You sure that's right, Dad? You're not rememberin some dream you had?"

"Look for yourself, if you don't believe me. It's under the bottom layer of meat." He started coughing again, so bad that Aaron paged the nurse, but his father recovered.

"Feel better, okay?" he said, standing to leave.

"Only if you look in that freezer."

"I'll be sure and do that, Dad."

He was walking through the door, thinking how delusional his father was becoming, when he bumped into the nurse entering the room.

"I'm sorry," he said.

"Don't worry about it."

Aaron had seen the nurse before, but had never really noticed her. Now he saw how her green eyes stood out against her brown hair. Although the scrubs hid the specifics of her figure, she still looked good. He guessed she was in her early thirties. He snuck a glance at her left hand as she stepped by him—no ring. *What the hell?* he thought. He hadn't spent much time with the opposite sex since his mother died six months earlier, then his father fell ill shortly afterwards. Dating a nurse, he could see his father regularly and still have something of a social life.

He stepped outside the room and waited for her to come back out. "I'm Aaron by the way," he said, offering an open palm.

"Gina," she said, shaking his hand.

"I was wonderin if you'd like to get a cup of coffee or go out to dinner some time."

"Sorry," she said. "I don't date patients, or their family members."

"It wouldn't have to be a date," Aaron said. "Think of it as me keepin you company on a break."

"Does that line ever work?" She looked annoyed, but maintained eye contact.

"Well," he said, grinning, "there's always a first time."

She laughed. "I'm on duty right now," she said, "but if you'll let me finish my rounds, I'll go have a cup of coffee with you in the hospital cafeteria."

"Sounds good to me," he said. "I'll meet you down there."

The hospital cafeteria was in the basement. A few people milled in and out, medical staff and family members of patients getting something to eat between rounds or before an all-night vigil. Aaron was sipping his second cup of coffee and had just finished a cinnamon roll when Gina sat down across from him.

"Sorry it took so long," she said. "The rounds in the cancer ward take a while."

Aaron nodded. "I'm used to waitin in my line of work."

"What do you do?"

"I'm a cop."

Gina didn't say anything for a minute, an awkward silence

Aaron had learned to expect from women when he told them what he did for a living. But Gina's silence was shorter than most. "So do you and your father get along?"

"We get along fine," he said. "Can I get you a cup of coffee?"

"Never touch the stuff. How are you taking his . . . bout with cancer?"

"I didn't ask you here to talk about my father," he said. "This is about me findin out more about you."

"Is this an investigation, officer?" she said, a coy smile flashing on her lips. "I can't ask you anything?"

"I just don't want to talk about my father at the moment."

"I'm sorry. He's an interesting man. He tells good stories."

"Has he told you about performin Elvis's autopsy?"

She laughed. "A time or two, yes."

"I can't believe how much he likes to tell that story. It almost ruined his reputation."

"What . . . you not a fan of The King?"

"You've clearly never had to work the beat durin Elvis Week."

"You got a point."

Aaron thought about mentioning the alleged liposuction, but realized if she had heard this version of the story, she would have undoubtedly mentioned it. Besides, he'd never heard the story before tonight, so what are the odds his father would tell a complete stranger about it?

They talked for half an hour, and Aaron said he would see her again the next time he came to the hospital. After a cordial goodnight at the elevator, Aaron drove to his father's house to see if he was telling the truth.

Aaron opened the door, walked through the darkened living room, turned on the light at the top of the basement stairs. He climbed down, and at first glance, nothing seemed out of the ordinary: various cardboard boxes with things like *kitchen*, *office*, and *breakable* written on the sides. In one corner were an old transistor radio and three giant stacks of LPs, many of them by musicians with whom Aaron was unfamiliar. There was a pin-up poster of an actress from the days of black-and-white movies, but he couldn't remember her name.

"Poor Dad," he muttered. "His girly-posters couldn't even show a little titty."

Near the back of the small basement, behind all the other stacks and covered with a moth-ridden quilt, was the deep freeze his parents had owned for as long as he could remember. He opened it and began removing packages of meat wrapped in butcher paper. At the very bottom was a stack of red plastic containers with the words *medical waste* stenciled on the side.

Aaron opened the top container and looked inside. The substance inside resembled human fat, but there was no way to know if this was what his father claimed it was from merely glancing at it. He replaced the lid and decided to take it to the chief technician at the MPD crime lab, a friend who owed him a favor. Aaron had saved him from an Internal Affairs investigation, so he could be trusted to keep things quiet, especially if his name was on the line. He took one of the containers, shut the deep freeze, and climbed the stairs. He locked the door behind him.

"I can't really tell you who this fat belonged to without expensive DNA testing and a lot of red tape," his lab technician friend said, "but I can tell you this—they liked pills, and a lot of them. Is this some new case you're working on?"

"Just somethin I'm doing for my dad."

"How is he?"

"Same as everybody . . . dyin a little every day."

"Sorry to hear that. If there's anything else I can do . . ."

Aaron slipped his friend a fifty dollar bill as he extended his hand. "I've got your number. See you around."

One of his cousins Aaron wanted nothing to do with had come up from Texas to see his father, so he found Gina and asked her if she'd like to join him in the cafeteria for a snack. Once again, the conversation turned to his father.

"Does he ever talk to you about dying?"

"No."

"Do you wish he would die?"

Aaron was appalled. "Why would I wish he would die? I don't hate my father."

"That doesn't mean you don't want him to die. Some people just want their parents' suffering to be over."

"You're completely off your nut."

She said nothing, but glared at him. She finished the rest of her meal without a word.

After Gina kicked his cousin out and pumped his father full of medicine, Aaron spent three hours watching network sitcoms with the sound off. He was about to leave when his father finally stirred.

"Dad? You awake?"

His father groaned a response, attempted to sit up in the bed, succeeded after four difficult tries.

Aaron scooted his chair closer. "I had a friend of mine in the crime lab check out that . . ." he searched for a word, "sample. He said whoever it was, he was popping pills like crazy."

"That was The King alright."

"Could belong to any hyper-obese pillpopper. I'm sure Elvis wasn't the only one of those you ever cut open."

"Yeah, but he was the only one whose fat I kept."

Aaron didn't say anything

"Smell it if you don't believe me." His father closed his eyes and laid his head back on the pillow.

"Hell no. I'm not smelling anything in a container marked *medical waste.*"

"Elvis smelled like fried fatback. The smell might have faded over the years, but I'd bet it's still there. My examining room smelled like a roadside diner for two months after he was in there."

"So by smellin the fat, I can determine that it actually belonged to Elvis. Sure, Dad, that sounds plausible."

Aaron could tell his father was beginning to fade back into the land of painkiller-induced catatonia. "Think what you will, but be sure and smell it to see for yourself," he muttered as his head slumped back into the pillow.

He told his father goodnight and walked to the nurse's desk. Gina was nowhere to be seen. He left the hospital in a foul mood.

Back in his car, he looked over at the container. He picked it up and opened it like a Tupperware bowl, waiting for the whisper of freshness.

His nostrils burned with the faint tinges of fried chicken, baked beans, peanut butter, bananas, and chocolate.

This is Elvis's fat, alright.

Aaron spent most of the next day cruising the streets in his police car. He didn't mind the work, or even the danger, but in a tourist city like Memphis, things could sometimes get out of control. His least favorite times of the year were Elvis's birthday and the week of his death. Elvis acolytes journeyed from all over to the Mecca of gaudy countryboy splendor: Graceland. RVs crammed to the gills with women who loved his movies, men who danced many a night away to his music, children who had never known him while he was alive but had received the proper Elvis culturing and were taking their final exams by visiting The King's mansion to celebrate the anniversary of his death. And the Elvis impersonators (as if there weren't enough of them in Memphis already) made the streets look as if Elvis actually *had* been an alien as the tabloids claimed and the rest of his race had suddenly invaded. Every conceivable variety of Elvis merchandise was hawked in every conceivable way, as if buying enough Elvis memorabilia would bring about the second coming of The King. Aaron loathed these people and the people who profited off them, taking their hard-earned money that would be better spent on a college education for their children or paying a little extra toward their enormous credit card debt and instead spending it on an Elvis commemorative spoon, a model pink Cadillac, a Bobble-Head Elvis that got "all shook up" at the neck and waist, Elvis cooking mitts, Elvis collector's cards, Elvis t-shirts, Elvis movie posters, replicas of Graceland, Elvis playing cards, and Elvis soap "so The King can clean every crevice."

After he got off duty, Aaron drove to the hospital, going immediately to the nurse's station. Gina wasn't on call. He kicked himself for not getting her number.

His father was watching the news when he entered the room.

"So did you smell the um . . ." he cleared his throat, lifting his eyebrows.

Aaron nodded. "It smelled . . . genuine."

"Told you so." His father laid his head back, closed his eyes. He looked more tired than Aaron could ever remember.

"So what should I do with all that . . . stuff?"

"Maybe try to make some money with it. That's why I saved it in the first place."

"What do you mean, 'try to make some money with it'?"

"Sell it, dummy. People will buy anything that has Elvis on it. Or in it. And I'm sure there are thousands of suckers out there that would sell their firstborn if they had half a shot at owning genuine Elvis fat."

"No way. I'm not one of those scumbags who makes money off a dead man."

"Then how do you plan on paying for my hospital bill? Do you think the insurance will cover all of this?" He waved his arm around the room. "Or Medicare?"

Aaron said nothing for several minutes.

"How would I go about sellin it? Nobody will believe that it's actually Elvis's fat."

"You tell them if they don't believe it, they don't have to buy it. But there's plenty of people out there who will buy it, just in case it really is."

"Isn't this illegal somehow?"

His father opened his eyes again. "It's not illegal to profit from stupidity. Besides, you're the cop, you should know that by now."

Aaron was wary at first. Sure, Elvis Nuts would buy anything— busts of Elvis, Elvis shades, Elvis key rings, a print of DaVinci's *The Last Supper* with Elvis in the middle—but he was afraid of offending the customers who treated Elvis with the seriousness and piety with which a Hindu would turn down a Big Mac. Still, he proceeded with the plan and four hours after he opened the bidding for an ounce of Elvis at onlineauction.com, the top bid sat at $475, with new bidders chiming in all the time. When the auction closed, Aaron was $1,100 wealthier.

The next auction for a vial of Elvis led to even fiercer competition between bidders. Since the bidding on the first vial had been so high, Aaron started the bidding for the next vial at $250. When the auction closed, an ounce of Elvis was worth $7,000.

Aaron decided he should start several auctions at once, giving him an opportunity to sell several ounces of Elvis at a time. By the end of the week, he raked in over $60,000.

Aaron was able to turn in his resignation to the police force, pay off his father's medical expenses, and live off his Elvis money within three weeks.

Aaron lay on his bed, enjoying the cool air from the fan blowing on his naked body. A light sweat covered him like fresh bedsheets. His last day on the force had been hot, made all the hotter by the black uniform he had to wear. To make matters worse, the air-conditioner in his care had gone out at ten o'clock, and he couldn't get it into a garage until four. By then, sweat had fanned out to the chest pockets of his uniform.

The air cooled the condensation covering his body, giving him a slight chill. He smelled disinfectant, which gave him an erection for no reason he could explain. Aaron sat up and asked the parrot on his bureau what time it was. The parrot told him to go fuck himself.

Gina walked in carrying a large bowl, licking the spoon she was scooping into it. "Pudding?" she asked.

"What flavor?"

"Banana," she said coyly. She scooped the spoon into the bowl and brought it to his mouth. She pulled the spoon out slowly, then popped it in her own mouth. The pudding's aftertaste was bitter in Aaron's mouth.

"Don't you like it?"

"It's okay. Not the best I've ever had, but not too bad."

She smiled, then dipped her hand into the bowl. She brought out a pile of the pudding in her hand, then smeared it all over her breasts. She dipped her hand again and rubbed it on her stomach.

Aaron put his lips on her nipple, licked the pudding off her breast.

"I need more pudding," she said.

"Later." He poked at her with his erection.

"I want more pudding," she said. "It'll be kinkier."

Aaron felt he could wait a few more minutes.

She returned only a moment later, holding a red container with *medical waste* stenciled on the side.

"I found what I was looking for," she said.

"That's not . . . pudding," Aaron said.

"It's where I got the first batch," she said. "It was in your refrigerator."

Aaron felt a gorge rising quickly in his throat. He ran for the bathroom, but it wasn't where he remembered. The hallway even seemed longer, and he didn't make it all the way to the end before falling to the ground and throwing up. His vomit was filled with chunks of fried food. When he finished heaving, he lay his head down, wiping his forehead on the carpet to get the sweat off.

Gina sat down next to him and covered the vomit with an orange towel. "Are you feeling okay?"

He could only groan.

She moved closer, taking his head and putting it in her lap. She began to caress his head, then worked her hands lower. Aaron's erection returned, and soon they were rolling over each other in a greasy mass of lovemaking.

The next morning he awoke in his bed, alone and confused, and set about changing his sheets.

It was strange to Aaron that he now thought of the containers marked *medical waste* in his basement refrigerator as Elvis memorabilia, not the leftovers of trying to squeeze a dead rock god into a morgue freezer. But it never seemed strange for long; watching his bank account grow as his mortgage, car payments, and hospital bills evaporated worked wonders on the repulsive thought that he was storing part of Elvis's remains where he had once kept his Bud Light. Though he had once loathed Elvis memorabilia collectors, he now felt a strange kinship to them. There were thousands of people out there who couldn't get enough Elvis fat, and he was making a fortune off them. No one who bought a vial asked if it was authentic or not, and anyone who asked questions wasn't going to buy a vial anyway, so Aaron never returned their emails. He had a good thing going, and no one was stopping him, so he did what any smart capitalist would do in his situation—he kept his mouth shut and let the money flow in.

Until the night The King showed up at his door.

II

It was well past midnight when his doorbell rang. Aaron was asleep, dreaming about all the things his Elvis money would bring him: a new car (anything but a pink Cadillac), new shoes (definitely *not* blue suede), maybe a trip to one of the other Elvis Meccas: Hawaii or Vegas. But whoever woke him with the doorbell wasn't letting up, and by-God wanted in.

Aaron slipped his Glock into one of the pockets of his terrycloth bathrobe, descended the stairs to his living room, looked through the peephole. A man wearing Elvis garb stood on the other side of the door.

Someone must have found his address and come to his home to harass him about making a profit from pirated Presley. But that didn't seem likely, since all the checks were sent to a post office box and Aaron had carefully concealed his identity online, so if anyone got too curious about the vials of Elvis fat floating around, the paper trail to him would lead nowhere. Apparently, someone had discovered a way around all his precautions and managed to track him down, coming to punish Aaron dressed as his Lord and Savior Elvis.

"I'm gonna give you to the count of three to get out of here," Aaron said through the door. "I don't take in Elvis impersonators after dark."

"I ain't no damn impersonator, man."

"You've got two choices the way I see it," Aaron said. "One, you can leave without making a scene and never come back. Two, I can pump your ass full of bullets and let you rot on my lawn. What's it gonna be?"

"Just open the damn door, man."

"One . . . Two . . . Three . . ."

Aaron threw the door open and fired a shot into the man's knee. He dropped down, but immediately stood back up. Aaron emptied the clip into his chest, knocking him back off the doorstep and into the yard, but he never fell.

"Damn, man, there ain't no need fer that," the Elvis said.

"Who the fuck are you?" Aaron wasn't sure if he was dreaming.

"I'm The King." When Aaron didn't respond, he continued. "You know? 'Ain't Nothin But a Hound Dog?' 'All Shook Up?' Graceland? Ringin any bells?"

"This is Memphis. Everybody and his step-sister is Elvis. Who the fuck are you really?"

Then the stench hit him. At first he could only smell gunpowder, but as the air began to clear, he noticed a much more ripe version of Elvis fat. His first impulse was to vomit and he tried to fight it off. However, as Elvis came closer, the smell got worse and Aaron spewed his guts all over the doorstep.

"I'm Zombie Elvis, back from the grave to take care of bidness. And your bidness is what I'm here to talk about." Elvis stepped past him as he was doubled-over and flipped on his living room lights.

The King has entered the building, Aaron thought as another wave of vomiting took over.

"Why you been sellin my fat?"

"How'd you know about that?"

"All the ruckus you raised done stirred up a whole mess of energy, so I redirected it into my body and come back to kick your ass." His voice was definitely Elvis's voice, though very dry and cracked.

"So you're what . . . a negative of Elvis?"

"No, man, I'm still Elvis, just in zombie form."

"So why are you back, if not to kill me?"

"Cause you sold my fat, man."

Standing under the light in the living room, Aaron got a good look at Zombie Elvis. Parts of his ears were missing, presumably rotted off. Rusted aviator shades covered his eyes, but failed to cover the skin hanging off the end of his nose. His lips had wasted away to reveal that Elvis now wore his trademark scowl permanently. His jumpsuit, once white, was now brown with earth and mildew around cuffs and collar. His gut (the part Aaron hadn't sold on the internet) sagged over a rusty dinner-plate sized belt buckle with the letters T C B emblazoned on it. His skin was gray and his hair, missing in patches, was the color of dead leaves with streaks of gray.

"My God, you've really let yourself go."

"Fuck you, man. You try fightin off worms and decay from beyond the grave."

"So . . . can I get you anything? Fry you up a mess of brains?"

Elvis ignored his question, stepped closer. He peered into Aaron's face.

"I'm gonna ask you again—why you been sellin my fat, boy?" His breath was unbearable, bringing tears to Aaron's eyes. He felt the contents of his stomach make ready for evacuation again.

Aaron tried to pull away from Elvis's horrible breath, but The King had the front of his robe in a firm grasp.

"Answer the damn question!"

"For money . . . I needed to help pay for my dad's hospital bill."

"Takin care of your daddy, eh?" Zombie Elvis's breath could turn the corners on wallpaper. "Well, I guess I can't get too mad about that. Now where is the rest of my fat?"

"In the basement."

"All of it?"

"Everything that hasn't been sold yet."

Elvis removed his glasses, and instantly Aaron wished he hadn't. The sockets were bare to the skull and the eyeballs, merely chewing gum stuck to a toothpick of nerves.

"How much did you sell?"

"Oh, I'd say . . . forty-five, fifty pounds worth." Aaron hadn't gotten the chance to really start shucking out the Elvis fat. He had been planning a big sale for the anniversary of Elvis's death in August. He still had a few weeks left to pump up the sale and really cash in on the Elvis suckers.

"Can you get it back?"

"I doubt it. Those people ain't gonna let go of their own little slice of Elvis."

"But it's mine. That's my fuckin fat, and I want it back." He poked Aaron's chest to emphasize the last four words.

"You can try, but I don't think they'll give it up."

"Even if *I* asked em to?"

"It would probably help, but then they'd all want to meet you."

Aaron's answer clearly agitated him. "That's the last thing I need, to be doin personal appearances at every damn fan's house. They'll invite all their friends . . ." Zombie Elvis, thankfully, turned his head. "I'll have to put on a show for all those people when all I want is to get back to my peaceful rest." He said nothing for a moment, then finally let go of Aaron's robe. "So where's the damn basement?"

"Follow me," Aaron said, being sure he stayed in front of the foul-smelling zombie.

"So that's all the rest of me?" Zombie Elvis asked, pointing a crusty three-ringed finger at the stack of medical waste containers in the refrigerator.

"All that hasn't been shipped."

Zombie Elvis pushed past Aaron and walked to the stack. He opened one of the containers and took a big whiff. "Oh mama, that smells delicious. Go get me a spoon, man."

"Do what now?"

"Just do it!" He spun, taking off his shades. Aaron took the stairs three at a time. He came back to the basement and handed the spoon to Zombie Elvis, who proceeded to scoop the fat down his throat. The spoon going into the container sounded like a wet fart, and as he slurped the fat down his throat, it created a sound like a vacuum cleaner in a sewer pipe. He finished one container, then started on another. Aaron felt his stomach churn, kept his nostrils pinched to keep the smell from overpowering him, and though he felt the urge to run, he couldn't peel his eyes away from the gluttonous eating habits of The King.

Zombie Elvis finished his meal after four containers. "Oh mama, I was definitely eatin some good pills back in them days." He tossed the spoon at Aaron. "Thank you. Thank you very much."

The spoon landed at Aaron's feet. "Don't mention it. Where you plan on stayin, or you just gonna kill me, haul all this fat back to Graceland and toss it in the fridge?"

"I ain't goin nowhere till I get it all back," Zombie Elvis said. "So until you get all the rest of me back, I'm gonna crash right here in your basement."

Aaron had been so busy with the Elvis fat business that he hadn't visited his father in over a week. Gina was sitting at the desk as he walked into the cancer ward. "Hey," she said, "haven't seen you around in a while."

"I've been busy with my new job." Aaron suddenly remembered the dream he'd had a few nights before, and realized he had not seen her since then.

"New job?"

"I'm in sales now. What are you doin for lunch? I'll tell you all about it then."

"I take my lunch break at two."

"Good. That gives me some time to visit with my father."

They made small talk for a few more minutes, then he headed down to the familiar hospital room. He entered and saw his father staring at the TV, but not really watching what was on the screen.

"Haven't seen *you* in a while."

He shut the door behind him. "I've been takin care of Elvis.

Literally."

"Is the fat sellin?"

"Not at the moment." He thought of Elvis chowing down on his own body mass and shuddered.

"But it has been?"

"Until Zombie Elvis showed up and started eatin it."

His father coughed without relief for several minutes. When he recovered, Aaron explained what had happened at his house several nights before.

"So he's pissed?"

"Hell yes, he's pissed. He's been sittin in my basement for the last couple days, chowin down his own fat. He's eaten up a lot of the remainin containers and wants to go after all the vials that have been sold, even though I told him there's no way those people are goin to want to give it up. But he says he's stickin around until he gets it all back."

His father sat in deep thought for a long time, saying nothing. Finally, he looked up and announced, "He should put on one last concert."

"Yeah, that's just what we need—'Come one, come all, see Elvis perform from beyond the grave . . .' Come on, Dad, get serious."

"I am serious. Elvis could give a final performance, and you could offer everyone who bought a vial a chance to meet The King after the show. They'll bring their vials to try to get him to sign them, and he can get them back from the people you sold them to and you'll be done with him forever."

"Are you sure people will fall for that?"

"They were dumb enough to buy his fat, weren't they?"

As soon as he got home, Aaron told Zombie Elvis about his father's plan for a farewell concert. "So what do you think about it?"

"You sure they're gonna go for it, man?"

"They buy all kinds of shit with your name or face on it. A lot of them have bought your fat, for Chrissakes, and I didn't even give them a certificate of authenticity. Why shouldn't they believe you can perform a final concert as a zombie?"

He stood, deep in thought, or what passed for it, for several minutes. "You got a point, man. When do we play?"

The next few weeks were the most stressful in Aaron's life. First, he tried to secure a venue for the concert to be held on the anniversary of Elvis's death, and there were already dozens of Elvis impersonator concerts scheduled for that day. His pitch for "the final performance that Elvis should have got" finally landed him a gig at a small club on the outskirts of Memphis. The place only held 350 people, but at least it was a place for fans to show up with their vials of fat.

The next problem he faced was finding a back-up band. The surviving Jordanaires weren't going to do it; a quick call to their agent revealed that they would cost a lot more than Aaron was willing to pay. He checked the alternative presses, hoping there would be a few rockabilly acts who might be willing to perform with the living corpse of The King. He had no luck for several days, but while reading the obituaries to his father, Aaron noticed an Elvis impersonator had died in a car crash. Aaron did a little clandestine research through his police connections and discovered the man was the singer for an aging Elvis cover band who called themselves The Stay Away Joes. He dialed the number his police buddy had given him.

"Hello?"

"I'm lookin for someone in the band The Stay Away Joes."

"I'm a Stay Away Joe."

"Would you be interested in playin a gig on the day of Elvis's death?"

"I'd love to, but we ain't got a singer no more," the man said, the sadness still heavy in his voice.

"I can provide the singer."

"You realize we only play Elvis tunes, right? And we ain't got no Elvis."

"I can provide you with Elvis."

"Yeah, but can he sing like The King?"

"The resemblance is uncanny."

There was a long pause on the line. "Let me talk to my fellow Joes. Do you have a number I can reach you at?"

Aaron left his number and the next day received a phone call informing him that The Stay Away Joes would play the gig.

"What songs can you play?" Aaron asked.

"Anything he ever released. Whatcha want us to do?"

"I haven't got it all worked out yet, but I'll call you when I know more."

Booking the venue had been hell and signing the band had been worse, but neither was as bad as trying to sell the tickets.

Like he'd done with the fat, Aaron set up a website to sell tickets to the show. He advertised proudly on his home page: "Buy a ticket to see the ABSOLUTE FINAL performance of The King EVER! On the anniversary of his death, The King will resurrect and play the last concert he never got to play. Tickets on sale now!" He emailed it to every one of his customers and to every Elvis website he could find. He added a link on the home page for Elvis fat customers, leading them to a page that read: "Have you purchased a vial of Elvis's fat from onlineauction.com? If so, you are eligible to meet Elvis after the concert! Be sure and bring all your vials of official Elvis fat so Elvis can sign them personally." Zombie Elvis had no actual plans of doing this. His wrists were so decayed that he could barely scratch an **X**. "Buy your tickets and get your chance to finally realize your dream of meeting Elvis!"

At first, Aaron's email filled with hate letters. People tried sending him viruses, media sources emailed him asking him all sorts of questions about how Elvis planned to "resurrect" and who he was trying to trick with this Elvis fat scam. Aaron read them, deleting the emails without replying. He had never forced anyone to buy anything. If they were willing to pay, he was willing to take their money.

Memphis Headlines:

ELVIS RESURRECTED: FACT OR FICTION?
IS THE KING REALLY COMING BACK?
ELVIS'S FAT: REAL OR HOAX?
LAST ELVIS PERFORMANCE: BEYOND THE GRAVE?
ELVIS TO GATHER FOR GRATEFUL...DEAD?

What a horrible pun, Aaron thought. But what did he care what they said? He was never going to have to work a police beat again, and Zombie Elvis would be out of his life forever. It was a good thing he could afford to buy a new house; the stench of Zombie Elvis was forever embedded into this one, although Aaron thought that might actually increase the value if he could sell it to an Elvis fan.

Ticket sales skyrocketed; all the negative publicity paid off. His venue was sold out less than two hours after the first news story broke, and emails were flooding in by the thousands demanding to know where they could get tickets and if there was any of Elvis's fat left for them. By the end of the week, representatives from Graceland were trying to negotiate an open-air concert to be held at the former home of The King. When they finally agreed to the price he held out for, he agreed to organize the Graceland concert.

Zombie Elvis spent most of his time in the basement, listening to his old albums and trying to decide which songs he remembered enough to sing. His voice wasn't what it had once been, but people couldn't expect his voice to be in mint condition after decades underground.

Zombie Elvis was beginning to run low on fat containers as well. He was eating three to five of them a day and as the concert grew nearer, the stack of containers grew smaller. Elvis's gut, however, was expanding at an unbelievable rate, and his hair grew darker and slicker. Even his skin was beginning to mesh back together, although it was still obvious to anyone who got a close look at him (or got within a few yards) that he had been dead and buried for a while. In addition to his own fat, Zombie Elvis had been chowing down on the peanut butter and banana sandwiches Aaron kept making to keep his uninvited guest happy. The King was truly becoming larger than life, the Henry VIII of Rock n Roll.

"How long you think you'll be able to play?" Aaron asked Zombie Elvis. "Hour? Hour and a half?"

"I don't know, man. I ain't put on no concerts in a long time."

"Well, what are you gonna try for?"

"I figure I might could give em an hour'na half, two hours if I feel up to it."

"And what are you gonna do afterwards?"

"I'll see em one at a time, get the vials back, and be done with it."

"And you really think it'll be that easy? They're just gonna hand over their own little piece of The King? And how long do you think that'll take, seein them one at a time?"

"I'll just take em out, one by one. I ain't in no hurry."

"Thousands of em?" Aaron laughed. "I don't think you realize your own power. Because you've been dead for so long, people could only get to you through your movies, or your music, or all that gaudy merchandise with you on it. Now that you're back and they've got a chance to see the real deal after you've been dead for so long, they're all riled up. And what would you do with their bodies? I think you've finally bit off more than you can chew."

Zombie Elvis sneered. "You got to think of somethin to do with them people," he said, "and you only got a couple more days. You best git to takin care of bidness."

Planning the Graceland concert was not as easy as Aaron hoped it would be. Trying to hire temporary staff members created more paperwork than he dreamed, and falsifying all the necessary information took a lot of time and energy. Ordering merchandise and food took up most of the rest. When he wasn't busy with the concert, he was trying to appease Zombie Elvis by making him "sammiches" or running errands. He had threatened to call the whole thing off, but Zombie Elvis laughed at him. "You done got yourself in over your head, man. Ain't no way you can call the thing off."

"There's got to be some way to get out of this. Maybe Dad has an idea."

Zombie Elvis snorted. "It's his damn fault you're in this mess. If he'd've let me be, this never would have happened in the first place."

Aaron wanted to tell Zombie Elvis that it had been his own fault that his father had lipoed him in the first place. He had been the one to take all those drugs, to eat all that junk food. He had been the one surrounded with sycophants who wanted him to look good so they would look better. If he hadn't been so fat and famous, and if his father had not been forced to perform the scandalous autopsy, his father would always be remembered as a respected medical examiner. But Aaron couldn't say any of those things. He had enough troubles with the Graceland concert without having Zombie Elvis pissed off at him. So instead he said he was going somewhere until he could think of a plan.

Because of the hours he was working and the amount of stress involved, Aaron's relationship with Gina was strained, at best. Though they often ate together, other than a few Friday night trips to the movies, they never went anywhere. Things were awkward between them when he managed to get down to the hospital. The dream he had a few weeks before still lingered in the back of his mind, and whenever he thought about it he shuddered. They talked a lot about his father, which bothered him, since he hoped to get some distance from his father's illness in his relationship with her.

"So I guess you've heard about the big Graceland concert, since you're a big-time Elvis man now." He was driving her home after dinner and margaritas.

"I'm actually workin with them to coordinate a few things."

Gina laughed. "You go from being anti-Elvis to working on the biggest Elvis event since he died."

"Elvis is big business, and it pays a hell of a lot better than bein a cop."

"Is he such big business that you can't visit your father a little more often?"

"What the hell is that supposed to mean?"

"You haven't been visiting your father as often lately. He says you're busy with work, but you were busy before and still made it down more than once a week."

"This happens to be the busiest time of year, Elviswise. Besides, it was Dad's idea."

"You want to know what I think?" There was a slur in her voice, tongue thickened by margaritas. "I think this whole Elvis thing you're doing is because you need to act out some unresolved issues with your father."

"Since when are you a psychologist?" Aaron said and instantly wished he hadn't—the margaritas must have worked on him too.

"Well, it doesn't take Freud," she said, the level of anger in her voice rising sharply with every syllable. "You hate Elvis and he has been such a major part of your father's life. You feel the only way to resolve the feelings you have of wanting your father to die and end his suffering is to overcompensate for hating Elvis."

"You don't have a fuckin clue what you're talkin about. And there is a hell of a lot more to my father's life than performin an autopsy on Elvis."

"You think you've got everything under control, but you have no idea how little control you actually have."

Aaron decided not to say another word until he dropped her off at her house. She slammed the door and he drove off, turning his vehicle toward the hospital.

Aaron shifted in his hospital seat, making the vinyl upholstery fart, but it did not appear to disturb his father's sleep. In fact, nothing Aaron had done or said in the last few hours had disturbed his father's sleep. The old man was quietly waiting out his last hours.

Aaron hoped his father would provide some counsel, as he had done so many times before. He didn't always agree with his father's advice, but he always welcomed it and more often than not followed the old man's suggestions. But now, when he felt he needed his advice the most, his father was comatose.

The television was on but the sound wasn't, casting an uneasy light in the otherwise dark, silent room. He tried to figure out how to deal with thousands of rabid fans who would be furious to find out they not only weren't going to meet Elvis, but they had given up their own small slice of him without realizing they'd never get it back. He figured the police detail assigned to work the concert would probably take care of the angry crowd with tear gas. Many of his former colleagues hated Elvis as least as much as he did, and the thought of gassing Elvis acolytes would probably thrill them. The crowd would go down and after some initial discomfort and confusion, go home dazed and a little ripped-off—no worse than any other concert.

He didn't think he'd have any trouble disappearing either. He had dealt with Graceland and the media through legal representatives—*It's amazing how many lawyers an ex-cop knows*, he thought. Once everything was over, he could quietly make his way out of Memphis at his leisure since no one knew he had orchestrated the entire operation. And with his hand firmly in the cookie jar of the Resurrection Concert, he stood to walk away with enough money to never have to wake up before noon again.

His biggest concern, though, was what would become of Zombie Elvis. He hadn't talked to Zombie Elvis about his plans for afterwards, and didn't really care what happened to him, just so long as he didn't have to see the smelly bastard ever again. But it was something that had to be thought out, since the thousands of people who would be cramming themselves in to see Elvis (especially the ones who expected to meet him) would be pissed off when he disappeared with all their fat.

Aaron wasn't even sure if Zombie Elvis would still be "alive" after the concert. Perhaps it was like a magic spell, where once all the ingredients were present the object would disappear. Or maybe Zombie Elvis could only go back to the afterlife after giving a resurrection concert for millions of rabid fans.

Aaron looked at his father, wishing the old man would wake up so he could at least give words of comfort and assurance if not advice. But Aaron got no comfort, assurance, or advice during this visit. He had to find his own solution.

III

Zombie Elvis was primping in front of the only mirror in the house.

There were lots of things Aaron was willing to give up because he was making money off Zombie Elvis, but the one thing Aaron would never forgive him for was the bathroom. The first time Zombie Elvis took a shit, Aaron understood why The King had died on his throne. When he wasn't rotting wallpaper with his rotten insides, Zombie Elvis spent hours staring at his own reflection in the mirror. Aaron was lucky to get five minutes to shave and brush his teeth.

"So what's your plan for when the masses revolt?"

"I plan on gettin the hell outta there, man."

"How do you plan to go about that?"

Zombie Elvis made a hoarse chuckling sound. "That's fer me to know and you to wonder bout, man."

Aaron called Gina two days after their fight. "I just wanted to say that I was a little drunk and didn't mean anything I said."

"I don't want to see you anymore," she said.

"How do you expect to do that? My father is a patient in your wing."

"Just don't talk to me unless it's an emergency. I was planning on transferring to a new ward anyway."

"Why are you doing this?"

"Enjoy your concert."

The phone clicked in his ear.

Zombie Elvis and The Stay Away Joes worked well together. Aaron had been worried about introducing the band to the zombified version of their idol, but although the smell kept a scowl on their faces for the first few songs, they eventually seemed to get used to it, the way a plumber grows accustomed to the stench of sewage. Their reverence for The King did not diminish in the least because of his monstrous form. They seemed content with the fact that he once more walked among the living.

On the way home from rehearsal, Aaron ran the air-conditioner full blast, but the stench of Zombie Elvis still wafted into his nostrils from the backseat where The King was stretched across.

"How many more of them containers you got in the house?" he drawled.

"Not many," Aaron said. "You've been hittin them pretty hard lately."

"It takes a lot of energy to perform. A man needs his vitamins."

"Was that what you told yourself when you were poppin pills like candy?"

Zombie Elvis sat up. "If it weren't for me, you'd be nothin. You'd still be walkin your shitty beat and wonderin how you can afford to pay the hospital bills that are buildin up while your old man's waitin to kick the bucket. Instead, you've got money comin in and all your problems are about to be over, and all you gotta do is keep me happy till I get all my fat back. It's just one concert, man. Can't you pull it off?"

"It's clear to me why someone else always handled the business side of things for you," Aaron said. "I've been bustin my ass to get back every bit of fat I sold and have been tryin to create this elaborate ruse to make you a star again for one night, and you treat me like your fuckin whippin boy. You have contributed not a goddamn thing to this event so far."

"You been bustin your ass because you gotta undo all the shit you did," Zombie Elvis sneered. "You could have left things alone, but you decided to stir things up, see if you couldn't get rich off the deal while you was at it. But you fucked up, so now you gotta pay your dues."

Aaron said nothing, realizing he had nothing to gain by arguing. He was sick of the entire affair. He didn't give a flying fuck about the concert. He had made his money off the fat and could do without the money from the Resurrection Concert, although he knew the event would make millions if he could pull it off. But was it worth the hassle? Was it worth giving up his dignity? If he could get rid of Zombie Elvis, then retrieve the fat from the people at the Resurrection Concert and sell it again, he could avoid the actual concert altogether, be free of the hassle and Zombie Elvis.

Aaron checked the rearview mirror. Zombie Elvis had stretched out over the back seat again, his aviator shades facing the ceiling of the car. Aaron slid his hand down under his seat. He gripped his pistol, adjusted it so he could quickly remove it from its holster when he got out of the car. He could dispose of the body without having to drag it far.

As he turned into the driveway, Zombie Elvis sat up in the backseat. "What if some of the people who ordered fat don't show up to the concert? What do you plan on doin about that?"

"They'll show up. Anyone who bought that shit won't miss their only chance to meet The King."

"And if they don't?"

"Why we arguin hypotheticals? There are enough things goin wrong with this concert already. So there might be two or three people who decide to hold on to their fat and not show up. What could it hurt you to lose a few pounds?"

Zombie Elvis got out of the car. "I ain't gonna warn you again about gettin smart with me." He started walking toward the house.

"All you gotta do is to keep bein Elvis," Aaron said as he reached down, removed the pistol, and got out of his car. "But in that direction." He raised the pistol, aimed for his face.

"What the hell is that supposed to mean?" Zombie

Elvis turned. Aaron fired and the shot hit Zombie Elvis in the shoulder.

Aaron raised the Glock to shoot again, but smacked his elbow on the door of the car and dropped it. He scrambled to recover it, but by the time he was ready to shoot again, Zombie Elvis had disappeared down the street. Aaron chased after him, into the darkness.

He fired twice when Zombie Elvis ran under a streetlight. The first shot missed completely, but Aaron thought he saw the second shot hit Zombie Elvis in the neck. When Aaron passed under the next streetlight, he no longer saw anything running ahead of him. Panting, he tried to find Zombie Elvis, but though his aroma hung in the humid air, there was no trace of him to be found.

People had been camping in front of Graceland for four days in preparation for what The Country Music Channel was calling "the event of the millennium." There was a parade at 10:00 that morning, littering Memphis with tons of crepe confetti. By 1:00 PM, the vendor booths around Graceland had fleeced millions off of people wanting to meet The King and witness his last live performance. Business was booming.

When the fat-exchange booth opened at 4:00 PM, Aaron was glad to see the line was long. He had always tried to imagine the people who bought Elvis's fat as lonely housewives, illiterate rednecks with a wistfulness for The Good Ole Days, and Southern *nouvea riche*. The people in line at the booth—as near as he could estimate, everyone who had bought a vial was trying to exchange it—looked like normal people, just wanting to trade their vial of fat for a backstage pass. Some resembled the stereotypical images that he'd had for Elvis fanatics, but most everyone standing in line looked like fine law abiding citizens who paid their taxes, phone bills, and tithes on time. There were people from the South, the North, from East and West Coast cities, a chartered bus carrying a fan club from Canada, a few couples from Europe, an old man from Australia, and even a Japanese man bearing a slight resemblance to The King decked out in *Jailhouse Rock* attire.

He checked the list of officers assigned to work security detail. To Aaron's chagrin, most of the officers had little to no riot experience. The department was not expecting a major disturbance from Elvis fans, perhaps a few drunk-and-disorderlies, standard to any large concert. They would probably be ill-equipped to handle an angry mob when Zombie Elvis didn't show. *But maybe,* he thought, *in the long run, that wouldn't be such a bad thing.*

Aaron hadn't seen the absentee star since trying to kill him again, and believed he had probably died from the injury. Even if he hadn't, he certainly wouldn't be able to perform after Aaron had shot him through the neck.

The Stay Away Joes were in their dressing room, some of them napping, the rest playing their instruments lightly. The ones that were awake looked up as Aaron entered.

"When's The King gettin here?" the guitarist asked.

"That's what I came to talk to you about. I haven't seen him in the last few hours. I'm not even sure he'll show up at all."

"What do you mean you're not sure he'll show up?" the guitarist stood, and the rest of The Joes awoke from their naps. "The King wouldn't miss his gig!"

"He could still show up," Aaron said, but they didn't believe him. "We had a bit of a fallin out last night after rehearsal."

"Well if there ain't no show, then we ain't stayin," the guitarist said and began to pack his equipment. "And we still expect to get paid. We got a contract."

"You can't leave yet. He might still show," Aaron said, but The Joes were not listening. They cleared the dressing room in less than five minutes.

Aaron stood in the parking lot, watching as The Joes' van disappeared from view. The concert was definitely off, and it was only a matter of time until the Graceland crowd found out.

Someone would announce the concert was cancelled and there would be a mob of angry Elvis fans who had been promised the performance of a lifetime. He decided he should retrieve the fat before the violence erupted.

He ran toward the fat exchange booth. The booth had closed half an hour earlier; the concert was scheduled to begin in five minutes, but Aaron knew he had some leeway, since he had never been to a concert that started on time. If he hurried, he could get the fat back to his car and be gone before anyone announced the show was off. He entered the abandoned booth and searched for the boxes of small vials. He couldn't find them anywhere.

Aaron ran for the backstage area, searching every crevice, opening every door to look for the missing fat or Zombie Elvis himself. He grabbed every technician and staff member he passed, asking them if they had seen anyone carrying boxes with glass vials. No one had seen anything. He didn't realize how long he had been looking until he heard the announcement over the PA that the concert was cancelled due to problems with the band.

A roar rattled the floor as the crowd voiced its disgust. Aaron decided escaping with the fat would have to take a backseat to simply escaping, then remembered his car was on the other side of the backstage area. The crowd was rushing the stage before he made it halfway there.

Some people were starting fires while others crawled over each other in a mad dash for anything that resembled an exit. Two sets of bleachers collapsed. The rookie cops were trying to maintain order by striking at people with their batons. Though he was winded, Aaron kept running. He burst through the door nearest his car, shut the door and locked it quickly. He gunned the engine and screeched out of the parking lot. The streets were crowded, but it was his only chance at getting away. He mashed the accelerator to the floor. In a stroke of luck, the street was clear to the right. Aaron twisted the wheel and sped toward the hospital.

Aaron barely made it to the cancer ward before the first big wave of patients arrived. The nurse at the desk (the only one left on the fourth floor) informed him that his father's condition was critical but stable. Aaron quietly shut the door to the room and sat in the chair next to his father's bed. The room maintained the strange quietness to which Aaron had grown accustomed, in spite of the chaos on the ground level.

He had no idea where Zombie Elvis was, and didn't really give a shit. He was reluctant to turn on the TV because he wanted to spend what could be his last moments with his father without any outside distractions. He could see the rise and fall in his father's chest getting fainter.

Someone tapped on the door.

Aaron froze. Surely no one could know he was here, and anyone who knew he was here wouldn't think he had anything to do with the Elvis concert. Except Gina, of course.

Whoever had knocked came in without waiting for a response. Aaron wrapped his hand around his Glock and pulled it free.

The nurse (not Gina) gave a small cry, but not enough to sound like she was genuinely frightened.

He put the pistol away. "How is he?"

"I'm afraid he's not long for this world. Have you heard about the big Resurrection Concert?"

"Not really," he said. "I'm not much of an Elvis fan."

"Apparently, the whole thing turned out to be a scam," she said, as if he hadn't spoken at all.

"That's what you get for worshipin a dead man," Aaron said.

"What a horrible thing to say," she snapped. "There are hundreds of people coming in critically injured, or even dead, and I'm sure there are a lot more on the way. Those people don't deserve what happened to them."

Aaron agreed to disagree. She finished whatever she had

come to do and left the room.

He sat down next to his father again, snapped on the TV. Fires at Graceland on channel 4. The same on channels 5, 8, and 11. He snapped the TV off again. *Well, at least I made it out without a scratch, even if I didn't recover the fat.* The entire place had been a fire hazard anyway. Nothing resembling orderly rows had been implemented during the concert. People had been too drunk on hooch, heat, and Elvis to stay in the bleachers. As far as Aaron was concerned, they had gotten what they deserved.

He felt a rumbling in his gut, and thought about how long it had been since he had been able to use the bathroom on a toilet that didn't reek of Zombie Elvis's rancid bowels. He walked to the bathroom, closed the door, sat down on the cool plastic seat.

There is nothing in the world as satisfying as a good shit, he thought.

He heard the door open and shut again, but thought nothing of it. *The nurse probably just forgot something.*

"So there you are, you sonofabitch."

Aaron would recognize that smell anywhere.

"I been waitin for this for a long time."

Aaron wanted to go out and stop him, but a turd was hanging out his ass. By the time he managed to get out of the bathroom, the door to the hall was shutting. He gave chase, darting out the door just in time to see Zombie Elvis step into the stairwell. Aaron ran for the door, but when he looked down the stairs, he saw nothing.

I'll take the elevator and cut him off.

He ran for the elevator and, in an amazing stroke of luck, it happened to be waiting on his floor.

When he got to the first level, he bounded through the halls, looking up and down for a fat zombie in a jumpsuit. The walls were lined with people holding bandages on cuts, scrapes, and burns of various degrees. Doctors and nurses were sprinting between rooms. He couldn't find Zombie Elvis anywhere. Paramedics blasted a gurney through a set of swinging doors; a charred Elvis impersonator screamed and writhed between them.

The sight of all the injured people reminded him that his father probably needed immediate medical attention. Zombie Elvis would have to wait.

As he turned to look for someone, Gina walked around the corner. He grabbed her by the arm and started pulling her toward the elevator.

"Dad's in trouble. Come quick!"

"I'm busy! There are patients everywhere!" She jerked her arm away from him.

"He's dyin, goddamnit!"

She stood still for a moment, looked down the hall, looked back at Aaron. "Let's go. But I'm doing this for him, not you."

They took the elevator. She didn't speak to him the entire ride.

They ran to his father's room. She opened the door and Aaron instantly heard the dull tone of a flat-line. Gina rushed to his father's side, checked his vitals.

"It's too late," she said.

Aaron couldn't say anything.

Gina looked at the equipment hooked up to the late James Priestly. "Someone cut the life support line," she said.

"It wasn't me. I heard someone in here while I was in the bathroom."

"You killed him, didn't you? You selfish shit!" She lunged at him.

Aaron stepped out of the way and ran for the door. Like Zombie Elvis before him, he turned for the stairs. Gina screamed and cursed behind him, yelling for the desk nurse to call security. It would be three minutes before she realized that the desk nurse was downstairs with the rest of her colleagues.

Perhaps it was because he had seen so much smoke in the sky recently that he didn't think anything was wrong as he approached his house. He was stopping by to get his bank records out of his desk, then going to the bank to remove a large sum of money from his account, skipping town to avoid Gina's accusations. After all, the money couldn't actually be traced to him and no one but Zombie Elvis, his lab tech friend, and his father knew that he was involved. He could go to Vegas, or maybe Cancun.

He turned onto his street and slammed on the brakes. Flames engulfed his house, creating a pillar of smoke in the early dawn sky.

He parked the car in front of his house. As he got out, he heard the approaching sirens of the Memphis Fire Department.

He couldn't believe it. After all he had been through, the money was supposed to make everything—living with Zombie Elvis, dealing with Elvis freaks, committing multiple crimes—worth it. Now the payoff to all he invested into his scheme was feeding the insatiable hunger of the inferno.

The fire engines turned onto his street and within minutes, firefighters were swarming around putting out his blazing home. Aaron could do nothing but stand by and watch, backing away as the roof collapsed. He heard a crunching beneath his feet, and when he looked down, he saw an old rusted pair of aviator shades lying in the driveway.

Tapeworm

SHE SUCKED IN AS much air as she could, and *stretched*. Almost. Again. Short by half an inch. The button would occasionally rub against the other side, but she couldn't quite get her jeans to fasten.

She lay back on her bed. Squirmed. Kicked her feet. She tried standing. A big, heaving breath, hoping upward momentum would lift her gut enough to snap the jeans. *The zipper will come up if I can just get them snapped*, she told herself.

Nothing worked. She sank back into bed. The trailer groaned on its wheels. Her last pair of clean jeans, and she couldn't fit into them. She would have to call in to work "fat."

Her mind did a quick inventory of the comfort food she had in the kitchen: cheesecake, Doritos, Little Debbies, Cheetos, Combos, Twinkies, double-chocolate fudge cookies, Ben and Jerry's, brownies. Then she remembered she didn't have the brownies anymore, after the sad movie she'd seen the night before on *Lifetime* and scolded herself because she knew comfort food would not help her situation.

She called work, told them she had a stomach bug. Got on the internet to search for a new diet.

She had already tried most of what she found: low carb, no carb, grapefruit, Atkins, Watkins, Simpkins, Tompkins, Weight Watchers, Slim Fast, DropItAll, binge-and-purge, torture-and-treat, lemon-and-prune juice, vegetarian (for a whole weekend), macrobiotics, microbiotics, regular-sized biotics, diet pills, Trimspa, the Hollywood Diet, the East LA Diet, Jenny Craig, Martha Stewart, Oprah, Dr. Andy's Miracle Weight Remover (which had kept her on the toilet for four days).

But no matter what she tried, her scales rolled easily over the 250 mark and were inching toward 300. She needed a quick fix, but hated knives, except for cutting steak. Or carving turkey. Or slicing a delicious chocolate cake . . .

She found a website offering a Victorian-era weight loss plan allowing you to eat as much as you want. The site sold tapeworm candy, promising the perfect hourglass figure of a corseted lady. There were before-and-after pictures of women who tried the treatment, transforming from Jenny Jellyroll to Jane Eyre in just a few weeks.

She pictured being nothing but lips, nips, and hips. Attracting handsome men. Seeing her feet again.

She retrieved her credit card from her purse. She might have a use for that comfort food after all.

Breaking Up Is Hard To Do

WHEN LEVI COMES IN, I'm cutting up a watermelon. Hey, hon, how are ya, he says, but it's not a question.

I know you're cheating on me, I tell him, not looking up. I saw the texts from your slut.

C'mon Char, he says, stooping down to pet my kitten, Mr. Mephistopheles. It doesn't mean anything. He leans in to kiss me. What's for dinner?

I stick the knife in his guts. It makes a wet, pulpy sound. I stab again. And again and again and again. I lose count.

His blood forms red storm clouds, creeping toward the dishwasher and soaking into the hair that he spends hours gelling and teasing every day. Already, in death I find him more interesting than he ever was in life. Mr. Mephistopheles begins to lap up his blood, red droplets staining his white whiskers. I wash my knife and go back to cutting.

Mr. Mephistopheles starts to meow, so I pick him up and help wash the blood off his face. We both have tuna for dinner.

The smell of Levi cooking fills the apartment. There's a knock on the door. His new girlfriend is in for a surprise.

Closing Time

MARY INVITED GLEN AND Brenda Frye to join them for their Sunday night after-church dinner at the Fish Nest, the restaurant Alvin owned. Alvin didn't like the Fryes—he always said Glen looked shifty and Brenda talked too much—but it was too late to un-invite them, so he was forced to sit through the conversation.

"It's so good to finally see you again, Sister Mary! I ain't talked to you in so long. How are y'all's kids?

"Our boy Brandon lives up at Malvern. He runs The Fish Nest up there. And Emma lives in Nashville. Her husband's a banker."

"Don't y'all have another girl?"

"Christie. She lives in Los Angeles."

"Oh really? What she do out there?"

"She's in pictures for makeup ads and sometimes shampoo."

"Oh my," Glen said.

"We raised her better than that, but you got to give em some slack, I reckon." Alvin pointed to his plate. "Mary, who's workin the kitchen tonight? This ain't done yet."

"I'm not sure," Mary said. "I think his name is Ed."

"Who runs this place when you're not here?" Brenda asked.

"Chuckie's our manager," Mary said. "I usually work whenever he has a day off, but Sundy nights are pretty slow, so we don't worry about it."

"So you don't do nothin here at the restaurant, Alvin?"

"I own it. I don't have to work here."

"He usually stays busy with his cows," Mary said. "He leaves the food business up to me."

When his order came back the way he wanted it, Alvin picked up the pepper shaker and shook it furiously over the baked catfish, covering it with a thick layer before coating the combination in ketchup. He looked around, caught the attention of a waitress rolling silverware, and waved her over. He touched her arm as he spoke.

"Scuse me, honey, what's the problem with the cook tonight?"

"He said the reason it wasn't right the first time was because he'd already turned everything off for the night before you guys came in."

"We came in at five till nine. Everything in the kitchen should be ready to go till closin time."

"They're just ready to go home. No one's been in since seven-fifteen."

"I don't pay them to wait around to go home, I pay them to keep the kitchen open till closin time. I'm gonna talk to Chuck about him."

"Do you need anything else?"

"Not right now."

"I don't understand the nerve of those guys," Glen said. "I mean, you pay em by the hour, right? Why should they mind stickin round a little longer while we eat?"

"Hard to get decent help," Alvin said, forking another bite of baked catfish.

The next week after Sunday night service, Mary invited the Fryes back to the Fish Nest. Chuck was working and took their order. Alvin ordered baked catfish the way he liked it. Chuck nodded and went back into the kitchen.

"I thought you said your manager didn't work Sundy nights," Brenda said.

"We had to get him to cover for the cook that got fired," Mary said. "It's only this week."

"He looks pretty young for a manager."

"He's twenty-four, but he's been working for me since he was seventeen," Alvin said. "One of the best employees I got."

Chuck put the food in the window and the waitress picked it up, brought it over to their table. A moment later Chuck came out of the kitchen, asked about the food, and went over to the front door. As he was about to lock it, the cook Alvin had told him to fire entered.

"Hey, Chuck. I thought I'd better bring back my shirts."

"Okay."

The cook looked over at Alvin's table, making eye contact with him. He handed his shirts to Chuck, then turned back to Alvin's table. He walked over, an old magazine in his hand. Mary looked down at her salad.

"I just wanted to say I'm sorry about messing up your fish last week, Mr. Strahand. But hey, no hard feelings, right?"

"Sure."

"I would like to thank you for something, though," the cook said, flipping the magazine open to the page where his finger had been stuck, "for having such a beautiful daughter who can run off to LA and pose for *Playboy*." The cook dropped the magazine on the table right between all their plates. Mary's iced tea spilled and started to cover the centerfold, soaking through airbrushed makeup and pubic hair. Ice spun across the page and came to a stop next to the words:

MISS MAY, CHRISTIE STRAHAND

"Night everybody. Enjoy your meal," the cook said, leaving through the front door.

Mary burst into tears and ran for the bathroom. Glen and Brenda kept their eyes on their plates. Chuck finally asked the waitress for some napkins.

"Chuck, get this thing out of here," Alvin said, pointing his trembling finger at the soaked magazine.

"Sure thing, Alvin." Chuck scooped up the *Playboy* and tossed it into the nearest bus cart, pushed it through to the kitchen.

"I think we'd better get on home," Brenda said. "Tell Sis. Mary I'll call later."

Alvin grunted and nodded. The Fryes stood and quickly left.

Chuck came back into the dining area, locked the door, and walked behind the counter to the register. "I didn't figure he'd come in at closin time on a Sunday night," Chuck said.

"Never know who you got workin for you these days."

"Is Mrs. Strahand okay?"

"I'll go see."

Alvin knocked on the door of the women's bathroom. "Mary? *Mary!* You got yourself together? It's time to go home."

"I'll be out in a minute."

He pushed the door open. Mary jumped back from the sink where she had been washing her face with a wet paper towel.

"Dry it up. Time to go home."

"Just a minute, Alvin, I'm tryin to get myself together!"

Alvin slapped her. Her head struck the wall of the nearest stall.

"Don't talk back to me, woman! Go get in the car."

Mary sniffled and walked out of the bathroom, Alvin trailing behind her. Chuck waved at them, barely glancing up from his ledgers and deposit slips.

"See you around, Chuckie."

"Sure thing, bossman."

The Artist and His Muse

HE FINALLY TALKED A girl into posing nude for him. He brought her to his studio apartment, pointed her to the futon while he prepared his pencils, his canvas.

"You do art here?" she asked.

"All the time," he said, biting into his bottom lip with deep concentration.

"Got anything to drink?"

He pointed her toward the fridge in the corner.

"What about coke?"

"Powder or liquid?"

"Either."

"Liquid, yes. Powder, fresh out," he said with some regret, but then added, "I do have some pot."

"That will do." She mixed herself a cocktail, took a shot out of the bottle before drinking it.

"Okay, I'm ready," he said.

"First the pot," she said.

They smoked a joint, and when it was his turn, she would take off a piece of clothing. He watched in leering interest.

When the joint was finished, he sipped at a beer and gave her notes on posture, the placement of her hair. His hard-on raged in his boxers. He traced her outline, removing his shirt. He shaded her curves, removing his pants. Her breasts were immaculate, her legs the kind you wanted wrapped around you constantly. As he carefully penciled-in her pubic hair, he began groping himself. He pulled his dick through the hole in his boxers.

"What the hell are you doing?" she asked.

"Admiring the model," he answered.

"You don't think I'm actually gonna sleep with you, do you?" She was sitting up, indignant. One hand covered her formerly not-shy-at-all breasts while the other fumbled for her clothes.

"Well, I thought it was understood." He wasn't flaccid yet, and she wasn't completely clothed. All was not lost.

"I thought you were some kind of art fag," she said. "I'm not actually interested in your tiny paint brush." She was walking toward the door.

"Come on, baby," he said. "I'm almost finished."

The door slammed shut behind her.

He was in tears when he finally came, wishing he'd taken a picture for reference. The drawing looked back at him disapprovingly, half-finished, a monument to failure.

The Ringing In Her Ears

*And if thy right eye offend thee, pluck it out,
and cast it from thee: for it is profitable for
thee that one of thy members should perish,
and not that thy whole body should be cast
into hell.*

— Matthew 5:29

BLYTHE AWOKE ONE MORNING with a ringing in her left ear—faint and faraway, almost unnoticeable. She even went in and did some modeling, and told anyone who asked her what was wrong that she had a headache. But the next day the ringing was worse, making it hard to even think, so she called in sick.

On the third day, Blythe went to see her doctor. The doctor examined her ear and started asking questions:

Had she been swimming in any lakes or streams?

Did she listen to music at excessive volumes?

Had she accidentally put anything in her ears lately?

But Blythe had done none of these things. The doctor wrote her a prescription for pills and a fluid to pour in her ear.

"What's wrong?" Blythe asked.

"I have no idea."

When the medicine had done nothing after five days, she called her doctor.

"The ringing is louder than ever and the stuff you gave me isn't working."

"I can schedule you an appointment with a specialist, but it will take at least a month to see him, so you should keep taking your meds until then."

"Thanks, doc. You've been *so* helpful."

She found she still couldn't do anything without the ringing in her ears breaking her concentration. She was too distracted to work, and couldn't watch TV or read anything for more than two minutes at a time. She tried to sleep, hoping she'd heal herself if she rested, but all she could hear was the increasingly louder ringing.

The idea seemed extreme at first, but after three days of thinking about it, she could stand it no longer. She marched into her kitchen, took out her sharpest knife, and cut off her ear. The ringing stopped as soon as the blade sliced through the skin. She bandaged it as well as she could, took three pills her doctor had prescribed, and slept peacefully for the first time in over a week.

When she awoke the next morning, she ran to the mirror and removed the bloody bandage, expecting the cut to be infected, or worse, hideous. Instead, she found it healed over completely.

Blythe rubbed her hands around the area, but it was as smooth as her cheek, not even a bump. She turned on her radio and found she could hear fine, so she spent the day listening to loud music, watching TV again, and calling friends she hadn't seen or talked to in a week. She decided to go in to work the next morning and went to bed early.

The shoot was in Stephán's studio, or as his neighbors called it, "the garage." Stephán was his *nom-de-plume*; when he'd gone to high school with Blythe, everyone called him "Steve." But after graduation he moved to New York and ran around with avant-garde photographers. When he couldn't make rent, he moved back to his aunt's garage apartment in Fayetteville. In the meantime he'd changed his name, insisting everyone refer to him as "Stephán." Blythe thought it was stupid, but since she also went by an alias, she didn't think he'd listen to her on the subject. Besides, he was a talented photographer, even if he was an asshole.

Stephán had no chance at making a living working only as an artistic photographer in Arkansas and refused to get a day job, so he started his own internet site and asked Blythe to model. He still considered his photography artistic, and refused to shoot straight nudity, always insisting she have an artistic element to her modeling. He'd tell her to cover herself in paint or pose as a statue that comes to life via a striptease. The website didn't make enough money for either of them to live comfortably, but it paid the bills and Blythe found the work empowering. Men all over the world gave up their credit card numbers and waited for her to post new pictures—rather, for "Lanie Carlyle" to post new pictures.

"Well, look who's finally on the set again," Stephán said. "Lanie Carlyle, back in the flesh—no pun intended of course."

"So what do you want to shoot today, Stephán? Are we doing Helen of Troy again?"

"Not today. I was thinking something more along the lines of—what the fuck happened to your ear?"

"I removed it."

"Bullshit. Is this some kind of Van Gogh joke?"

"No, it was bothering me and the doctor wasn't helping, so I just got rid of it."

"Are you out of your fucking mind? You can't be in porn missing an ear. That's *weird.*"

"What do you mean, weird? I would think that weirdness would make porn more appealing."

"Sure, you could go for that amputee fetish market," Stephán said, chopping the air with his hand. "But you'd need to be missing an arm or a leg or something normal like that. The only way you could have done worse was cutting off a tit."

"What are you talking about?"

"Let me tell you something, Blythe—no guy wants to jack off to a girl missing an ear."

"Let me tell you something, Steve—I quit. If you're going to be an asshole about this, then you can go find a *normal* girl to pose for you."

He was still stammering when she slammed the garage door.

Getting a new website started was no problem—Lanie Carlyle had developed an online following who, despite Stephán's suggestion, didn't seem to mind her removal all that much. Her website had stolen most of his subscribers within a month.

Before long, Lanie's page was becoming one of the most popular adult sites on the web. Her email account soon flooded with offers and one afternoon, as she browsed her various opportunities, she noticed something dripping from her nose. She swiped a hand over her upper lip and looked down at her fingers. They were covered in blood.

Rather than call her doctor again, Blythe went to SelfMD. com. She typed in her symptoms and sent them through the database. The results were inconclusive.

Blythe searched the web again and tried every home remedy she could find to keep her nose from bleeding. She tried twisting the ends of tissues and keeping them up her nostrils, but the tissues soaked through. She tried keeping her head elevated, but the blood streamed down her cheeks. She tried blowing her nose to see if she could somehow exorcise the cause of the bleeding, but it kept flowing, as if she found a fountain of red wine between her sinuses.

When she ran out of ideas, she got her bandages and knife. Five minutes later, she was wearing bloody gauze across her face.

The next morning when she went to change the gauze, she expected to see a gaping hole in the middle of her face. She'd lain awake for hours, wondering if she'd ended her modeling career with the quick swipe of a knife. But when she took the bandage off, she found it had healed completely, except for two small holes just above her upper lip. She could breathe fine, and her face simply went flat.

Two days later, she was posing again. Within a week, she had almost doubled her subscribers. By the end of the month, she was getting emails from girls wanting to pose on her page. Imitators began springing up all over the web, but none had the aesthetic of Lanie's site—their amputations were often ghastly; Lanie's removals looked as if someone had simply erased parts of her body.

After a month of getting used to life with her new removal, Blythe began to notice a pain in her left shoulder, probably from playing tennis at the athletic club.

She typed up a poll and added it to her daily blog: *Would you like to see Lanie Carlyle subtract even more of herself?*

When she checked the poll results a few days later, she found the majority of her subscribers supported her new removal. There were even emails with suggestions—one guy emailed her four times about poking out an eye.

The checkout clerk at Home Depot was ogling at her as she set the hacksaw on the counter. "Doing some home repairs, miss?"

"Something like that." She tossed her credit card down and wished he'd stop staring at her. She was fine with millions of men staring at her boobs for hours a day, but couldn't this guy take his eyes off her face for fifteen seconds?

By the time the clerk ran her credit card, almost all the clerks in the store were leering at her. When the customers started turning and gawking as well, Blythe felt like picking up the hacksaw and running for the door. But she resisted, and walked out of the store with her head held high. *Fuck em*, she thought. *They probably hate their jobs.*

She was modeling again the next afternoon, announcing to all her subscribers that Lanie Carlyle had removed another body part.

Her ear was ragged, scabby. Her leg looked like someone had twisted it off above the knee. She removed her prosthetic nose, leaned down to the compact, and snorted a line of coke.

"Want some?"

Blythe shook her head. "I've got no nose for the stuff."

The girl giggled. "I get it. You know, I really admire the way you do your thing."

Blythe smiled at the girl, another one of the hopeful contestants for the reality TV show she'd agreed to do. She was surprised at the number of women willing to compete for a free body part removal and a modeling contract with her site.

"It's amazing how many of my problems went away when I started using a knife," the girl said, replacing her nose as she stuffed the coke in her prosthetic leg and hobbled for the door. "Thanks for showing me the way, Ms. Carlyle. See you on the set."

Blythe said nothing and adjusted her own recently acquired prosthetic leg, thinking about how many of her own problems she'd solved with a knife—first the ringing, then the bleeding, then the pains in her extremities. A knife had taken care of everything so far, except for the migraines that had started to plague her.

Arson: A Love Story

I HOLD A PICTURE of Deanna in my fingers. Its edges are starting to wear away, but she is as beautiful as she's ever been. I take a deep breath, and continue to wait for her.

She looks deep in my eyes, and asks me if I love her.

Of course I do, I tell her.

Then do this with me, she says.

There's the strike of a match, and sulfur and gasoline fill my nostrils.

The doctor enters the room. He tells me his name but I'm not interested, so I forget it instantly. They tell me you've been having headaches, he says in my direction.

I shrug.

Do you have one now?

I shrug again.

What do you have in your hand?

I put the picture of Deanna in my pocket and say nothing, even though he insists on seeing it.

We make love in the firelight. It's no candlelight dinner on a moonlit beach, but we both find it a highly romantic setting.

There were people in that home, the doctor tells me.

I know, I tell him. Just like I know what they did to her, the extent of their abuse.

Who? he asks. This Deanna you keep going on about?

You'll never find her, I tell him. I won't let you.

The last time I see her, she's getting dressed in a hotel room, several hundred miles from where her parents lay, charred and ashen. We can't be seen with each other for a while, she tells me. It's too suspicious.

Will you wait for me? I ask.

Of course, she says, leaning down to kiss me. I will wait for you as long as it takes.

The doctor is insistent that Deanna does not exist, so I show him her picture. If she's not real, I say, then who is this?

It could be a picture you stole, he says. We can find absolutely no record of her.

Then she's done an excellent job of hiding, I say.

The police arrive twenty minutes after she leaves. They tell me the manager suspected something when she smelled gasoline and smoke coming from the laundry room. They arrest me for arson.

I tell them they will never find her. I tell them over and over again.

So where is she hiding? the doctor asks me. Why haven't they found her yet?

Maybe they're not that good at their jobs, I suggest.

He sighs, writes something down in his notebook.

Maybe she doesn't want to be found.

He writes more.

But she's waiting for me, I tell him. When I leave this place, we will be together again.

He closes his notebook. I think I've done all I can, he says, not necessarily to me.

Deanna has eyes the color of Christmas trees. Her lips make a Cupid's bow and give the softest kisses in all human history. Her hair is the color of flame and when she dances, it looks as if her shirt has caught fire.

She gives me a picture of her. It's not a very good one, she says, but it's the only one I have.

Any picture of you is a good picture, I tell her.

The headaches start the first time I meet my lawyer. I wince as he walks into the cell.

Are you feeling okay? he asks, no actual concern in his voice.

I'm fine, I tell him.

Is there anyone who can confirm this story about the people in that house abusing your girlfriend?

Deanna, I tell him. Deanna told me all about what they did to her. She said it was the only way to get back at them.

I've looked all over for her, the lawyer tells me. The investigators can't find any trace of this woman. There's no proof that she ever existed.

I have her picture, I say. I show it to him.

I'm pleading you not guilty by reason of mental defect, he tells me.

I shrug. Do what you have to, I tell him.

He stands to leave. I ask him for an aspirin. He says he'll see what he can do.

After we make love, Deanna cries. I ask her what's wrong, and she tells me about what her parents did to her over the years. How she had run away many times, had always been brought back, and the abuse got worse and worse. I hold her close, feel her tears soak into my skin.

We'll get revenge, baby, I tell her. I tell her over and over again.

She shows me the house. I nod. We buy gallons of gasoline, a box of matches. We have a picnic dinner behind her old house.

We'll strike when the moon is high in the sky, she tells me.

I nod.

The headaches get worse every day I'm away from Deanna. I will wait forever if I have to, but I must be with her.

The lawyer visits my cell again. He tells me what the doctor told him, but I can't concentrate through the pain. He says I'll probably not end up in prison. I tell him life without Deanna is prison, and one day, soon, she will come and set me free.

We get as far away from her old house as we can, even before the firefighters arrive. We spend a few days on the road. We make love in hotel rooms. We are in love.

They take me into a small room, with a small bed and a small window. Too small to climb through, too high to reach unassisted. They take away belts, shoestrings, bedsheets, but they let me keep my picture of Deanna.

When they leave, I study her picture. I memorize her every feature. As I do, the headache subsides. Somewhere, out in the wild free world, she is waiting for me.

Whore of Babylon

I

*Come hither: I will shew unto thee the judgment
of the great whore . . . with whom . . . the
inhabitants of the earth have been made drunk
with the wine of her fornication . . .*

— Revelations 17:1-2

IT WAS A SUNDAY when I first saw her. I was out with the congregation of First Church of the Pentecost, handing out tracts to stop the murder of the unborn, and happened to look up at a billboard. I didn't mean to; I tried handing a pamphlet to a woman and she shoved me out of her way. When I looked up for guidance from The Lord, there she was.

She had long blonde hair and lips redder than Jezebel's. She wore almost nothing and just outside her mouth were the words:

BABYLON IS COMING

Her long legs took up the rest of the sign.

I must confess that when I first saw this sign, my thoughts were not on God but on the flesh. It wasn't until I felt the flesh rising that I realized The Devil was tempting me with his trap of lust, and recognized the sign for what it was.

I forgot about passing out tracts and headed home. I had more urgent work to do now.

Reverend Baker was not so clear on the sign.

After church that night, when I was shaking his hand, he asked me why I hadn't finished the Sunday afternoon crusade. I told him God had given me a vision and I had gone home to start making ready for His return.

"Oh, Brother Simmons, don't you remember the Bible says he will come as a thief? What makes you think you saw a sign?"

"Because I did see a sign. You can see it too."

"Where?"

"State Line Boulevard."

So we drove down State Line. I pointed out the billboard. He laughed.

"It's an advertisement, Jody."

"It's the Whore of Babylon."

"Babylon is just their product, Brother Jody. Tell you what you should do. Go home, read the Book of Revelation again, and pray about it real hard. See what God is trying to tell you."

I didn't bother telling him I had spent the rest of my afternoon rereading Revelations and the entirety of his sermon, praying silently about the sign. I just let him get back in his car and drive back to the parish. If God wanted to test my faith, He would be my strength.

> *that woman Jezebel . . . calleth herself a*
> *prophetess, to teach and to seduce my servants*
> *to commit fornication . . .*

> — Revelations 2:20

I couldn't sleep that night. All I could think about was the naked woman on the billboard. Why couldn't Reverend Baker see her for what she was? *Those pouty lips, those long tan legs, the cleavage peeking out over the main street of the city* . . . she was only here to distract men of God. But every time I tried to forget her, her breasts would peek out at me from the small bikini top that had been burned into my skull. I prayed to God for strength, to take this burden of lust from me. I closed my eyes as tight as I could and tried to will her seductive power away—if I fell, who would carry on?—but whenever I thought it was gone, the billboard would pop into my mind again. The spirit was willing, but the flesh was more willing, so eventually I gave in to temptation, I'm ashamed to admit. But as soon as I'd finished, I got on my knees and asked God for forgiveness, even before I went to the bathroom to wash away the crust of my sin.

The man at the UPS Store looked at me strangely when I went to pick up my fliers, but I didn't care—when I was among The Chosen and he was burning eternally with The Damned, he'd remember his missed opportunity for redemption.

My boss looked at me even more strangely when I told him I wouldn't be working for him anymore. He didn't seem to understand the importance of my spiritual work and why I could no longer work at the tire factory. I told him I didn't have forty hours a week to spare, and handed him one of my fliers, explaining to him the significance of each verse and how they had already come to pass. I told him about the Whore of Babylon on State Line, how he could see the most recent sign for himself. He shook his head and said I was overreacting. I told him I would pray for him, and that I forgave him, even though God probably wouldn't spare His Wrath on Judgment Day. He said he'd send my paycheck in the mail and asked security to escort me out to the parking lot very politely.

Standing on the pavement all day was hot work, but I kept reminding myself if I didn't burn up a little now, I'd burn for all eternity. So I stuck with it, handing out fliers to everyone who passed, pointing to the billboard so they could see for themselves. Most of them took the fliers and kept walking, but God knows how to trouble their hearts.

Texarkana police from both sides of the line showed up a few times my first week, but when I told them about the Whore of Babylon on the sign, they just told me not to harass anyone too much and stay out of trouble. The cops were really nice guys.

At the end of the first week, I saw some billboard workers climbing the Whore of Babylon sign and thought maybe someone had gotten my message and was changing their ways. I decided to take some time off, maybe get a sandwich and a Coke at the Subway down the block to celebrate my victory for Christianity. But when I came back, I saw that, if anything, there was much more work to be done.

The Whore of Babylon had on only a pair of bikini bottoms, her breasts barely covered by a bottle of beer. Over the top of them both:

BABYLON IS HERE

> *For the great day of His wrath is come; and who shall be able to stand?*

— Revelations 6:17

No matter how hard I tried to fight it, I couldn't get the image of the woman on the billboard out of my mind. You could practically see her whole tit, except for the beer bottle. *The curve of her body compared so blatantly to the bottle . . . the sweat running down both of them*

. . . her full red lips . . .

And then I was praying for God's forgiveness again, and for strength to fight His battles. How was I supposed to be a beacon of light for Him if He couldn't help me control my sinful urges?

Then I asked forgiveness for questioning His mysterious ways.

I was in Wal-Mart trying to decide between two different markers for the posterboard I was buying, when I heard someone in the next aisle talking about the Babylon girl. I peeked around the corner and saw the Whore of Babylon herself, in Wal-Mart, talking to a man and autographing something for him.

"I haven't had the chance to try it yet, but I love the sign," he said.

"You know, I haven't tried it yet either," she said. They both laughed. He thanked her and went back to looking at cookware. She kept walking down the aisle.

I left the posterboard and markers on a shelf. God was speaking to me as I followed her through the checkout and into the parking lot.

By the time she pulled into Babylon Brewery, I knew exactly what I had to do.

She got out of her car, started putting her keys in her purse, but dropped them. As she was trying to pick them up, I got out of the car and walked over. When she stood up, I handed her one of my fliers.

"You should have a look at this."

She scribbled on the flier and handed it back to me without even glancing in my direction. "Thanks. Have a great day." She turned and headed for the factory.

"No, I need to talk to you." I grabbed her elbow, just to slow her down.

"Hey, jerkoff, let go of me!" She reached in her purse and

pulled out a can if pepper spray.

The Lord must have been working through me because before I knew what was happening, I had punched her in the stomach and she was rolling on the ground.

I looked around, but no one was outside. Even with God on my side, I knew I would have trouble explaining this situation to anyone who happened upon us. So I decided to take her back to my house to witness to her one-on-one.

She struggled getting into the car, but I punched her a few more times and she traveled easily. I was back at the house and had her strapped to a chair in my garage before she came around.

I retrieved my Bible from inside the house, and when I got back she was yelling for someone to help her. I raised my hand to slap her and she shut up. I read passages from the Book of Revelation to her, but she didn't seem to understand, so I smacked her with the Bible.

"Pay attention! I'm trying to save your soul!"

"Please, mister! Just let me go! I haven't done anything!"

Clearly she wasn't listening to me, so I read more passages from the Bible. I told her about the seven seals, how men were tempted to commit fornication and get drunk, how the signs of the times were upon us and how her unwitting support of The Devil was damning her soul.

"Now do you see what you're a part of?"

"I'm just a model, mister. I'm just a goddamn beer girl."

I slapped her for blaspheming in my house, even if it was only the garage.

"*You*," I told her, "are the Whore of Babylon, and *you* are bringing on the Reign of the Beast. You're a predecessor to the Antichrist. *Now* do you understand why I'm trying to save you?"

She only sniffled. There was blood flowing down the side of her mouth.

I kept reading her passages, hoping she would come around. Tears streaked down her cheeks, but she didn't say anything else.

I decided to give her a chance to sleep on the state of her soul, grabbed a rag off my workbench and stuffed it in her mouth. She started to shriek when I went to put it in but I threatened to turn off the light. The gag suddenly didn't seem so bad.

And in her was found the blood of prophets
and of saints and of all that were slain upon
the earth . . .

— Revelations 18:24

I didn't get much sleep that night. I prayed a lot—she didn't seem to want to repent, and I wasn't sure how much longer I could keep this up. I didn't like being violent, but once the path was taken, it had to be followed to its end. After all, these are the End Times and I can't screw up my duty to God so close to the Rapture. Nothing The Devil would like more than to make me fall so close to completing my task.

Of course he was tempting in peak form. He sent me thoughts about her in the garage, too weak to fight back. *Touching her hair, stripping her down to see what the billboard had not revealed.* I prayed for deliverance. The thoughts dissolved.

She repents, falls in love with me for showing her God's Way. We get married, and in the marital bed I have her, the one so many had desired . . .

That wasn't right either. If God *chose* to give her to me as a reward for doing His Divine Plan, that was one thing. To wish for such a thing was selfish.

Lust adequately defeated, other thoughts crept in: What if someone had seen her in the car? What if there were cameras in the parking lot? What if she managed to get free and escape?

I tossed and turned, occasionally getting enough fitful sleep to dream of opening the garage and finding it empty. As soon as I awoke I went downstairs to check on the Whore of Babylon.

Her eyes were wide when she saw me. She was sweating and trying to talk through the gag.

Even bruised, dirty and bloody, the Whore of Babylon was still a very beautiful woman.

I removed the gag. Her voice was hoarse.

"Please, mister, I want to repent. I realize what I done, and I want to make it right with Jesus."

I closed my eyes and was about to thank the Lord when the doorbell rang.

The Whore's eyes lit up, but I replaced the gag before she could scream.

Reverend Baker was on my front stoop.

"Brother Jody. I hope I didn't wake you."

"I was just getting up. Would you like to come in?" The invitation came out before I could stop it.

"I'll only stay a minute or two." He stepped into my living room and walked through to the dining room table. "I suppose you'll be heading off to Cooper Tire shortly."

"I'm not working there any more."

"Well, what are you up to these days?"

"I'm starting a spiritual campaign."

"What kind of campaign?"

"It's still in its beginning phases."

"Is that why you haven't been to the last few services?"

"Starting a ministry is hard work, as you well know."

"But it's no excuse to separate yourself from the rest of the flock. I'd like to see you back in the pews, Brother Simmons. For your own good. God wants you to know that you're part of a community of people who love you."

"I know that, Reverend. I talk with God all the time."

He pulled a yellow piece of paper out of his pocket. I recognized it before he got it unfolded.

"Do you know anything about this, Jody?"

"I know what God tells me, and what I read in my Bible."

"Have you read what the Bible has to say about false prophets?"

"You never believed in the sign in the first place." I wished he would leave. I had enough on my plate without the preacher coming around asking me why I hadn't been to church. "So why should I trust you when God tells me different?"

He put the flier back in his pocket. "I just hope it's God's voice you're hearing, Jody."

I told him I had to go. He said he hoped to see me in church and turned for the door to the garage. My heart nearly stopped, but I pointed him in the right direction, right before his hand reached the doorknob. He had trouble with the front door, so I gave him a hand opening it.

Through the window, I watched his car pull away, keeping an eye on my street for several minutes. Satisfied no one was spying on me, I walked back into the garage, removed her gag, and asked if she meant it when she said she wanted to repent.

"Oh yessir, I sure do. I realize I've been living in sin, and I want to get right with God so I can quit working for The Devil."

"Do you know how to pray?"

"A little."

"Then bow your head and let me hear you."

She whimpered apologetically about sex and drunkenness and drugs and lots of other stuff and said she wanted to start her life over again but right this time for Jesus sakes amen.

She looked up at me eagerly.

"Don't you feel better already?"

She nodded.

"Come, sister," I said, loosening her restraints, "I'll help you find the way of Christ."

She read the Bible aloud at the table while I cooked breakfast for the two of us. I'd shown her the bathroom and lent her some of my clothes, and though The Devil tempted me to watch her in the shower, I'd pushed the thoughts away.

"What made you realize who I was?" she asked, looking up from the scriptures.

"It was like a vision. I looked up and God just spoke to me— *That's the Whore of Babylon.*"

"That's amazing. I think He must really have a plan for you and me."

"He's got a plan for everyone."

"But us especially." She put her hand on mine. "I think God wants me to be your wife, and for me to help you in your mission."

I was sure this was my reward for converting her. I thanked God and took her in my arms. Then we were kissing, rolling around on the floor.

I could feel my pants tightening, her tongue in my mouth. My hand was squeezing one of her breasts when I remembered a passage from the Book of Revelation: *These were they which were not defiled with women . . . redeemed from among men . . . and in their mouth was found no guile: for they are without fault before the throne of God.*

I pushed her from me. "Wait, I don't think I can—"

That's when she smashed a lamp over my head.

I was stunned for a moment. My forehead was wet, fingers red. The Whore was off the floor, headed for the door. I staggered to follow.

She had trouble with the lock, took too long to figure it out. She got the door open but before she could get off the stoop, I grabbed her long hair and pulled her back inside, bolting the door behind me.

She kicked at me and bit my arm when I put her in a headlock. She reached for a table fan but I rammed her face-first into the wall. Straddling her chest, I put my hands around her throat.

For an agent of the Antichrist, she didn't put up much of a fight. It wasn't long before she wasn't breathing anymore.

I loaded up the car inside the garage after dark. When the last light on my street went out, I drove the thirty-four miles to the

Red River County Landfill.

On the backside of the dump, I took out my shovel and dug up a mound of trash and red clay. When I had moved enough garbage, I dropped the dead Whore of Babylon in the middle, then covered her with the filth she deserved. The sun was peeking over the horizon, God looking down on the good work I'd done.

II

*For He hath judged the great whore, which did
corrupt the earth with her fornication . . .*

— Revelations 19:2

It was a beautiful morning, and the gospel radio station was playing instrumental hymns flowing into each other on a piano.

If I hadn't seen the sign on my drive home, I wouldn't have even thought of her.

But I did. And not the way I used to. But I did think about that too, as I lay in bed, trying to fall asleep. The Whore had involved much more labor than I'd expected, and after not working at Cooper Tire for a few weeks, I'd quit exercising, so carrying her around, the digging and everything, pretty much wore me out. I figured I'd be snoring in no time.

I contemplated the red 9 on my clock so long it turned into a 10.

Had I done God's Will? I prayed, asking Him for guidance, to keep away those who would stand in the way of His Divine Plan.

God is very subtle, so I didn't expect immediate answers, and was not disappointed when they didn't come. But I felt better having spoken to Him, and remembered that if I expected Him to help me, I'd have to help myself.

Ashdown is twenty miles north of Texarkana and while I know a few people who live there, the nearest Pentecostal church was fifty miles away in De Queen, so I didn't think I'd run into anyone who wanted to have a chat, peek in the cart, and tell me the latest church gossip while taking notes to pass to the next church person.

My list looked harmless: soap, matches, bleach, trash bags, paper towels, carpet cleaner, scrub brush. I also bought a printer/

copy machine, several boxes of paper, and a design program for my computer. I was tired of the guy at the UPS Store glaring at me all the time.

When I got home I cleaned the bathroom, kitchen, and living room. I tried to remember if she'd been in the bedroom—it'd be just like her to try leaving something behind—and cleaned it anyway, just in case. I put the clothes she'd been wearing and the stuff I'd lent her in a trashbag, then stripped naked and added my own clothes and bedsheets. Then I vacuumed the car and scrubbed the trunk until my fingernails chipped.

At some point I awoke with my head resting on the chair in the garage, a rag in one hand with a bottle of degreaser tipped over and pooled around my ankle.

When I tried to install the design program on my computer, I discovered how little I really knew about computers. I spent an hour on the phone with the staff at Wal-Mart, who finally gave me the number of the manufacturer. Their service hotline kept me on hold for forty-five minutes, sent me around the staff, then apologized for not being able to help after an hour and a half.

I took the program to a local computer store, where the service rep stared at the box, went in back and left me to stare around the store for twenty minutes. I tried not to get angry, realizing God must be trying to tell me something. I thought about how many people it was taking to do something as simple as install a computer program, then my mind turned to church. I decided God must be telling me to go back. If I was going to do His Work, I needed them on my side. Plus the preacher would think his talk did me some good, and it never hurt to have him on my side.

My mouth always gets dry when I have to speak in front of people. It's why I was never in the choir—I'd get halfway through a song and I'd be choking and coughing, running for the water fountain at the back of the church.

But I didn't have a choice. I had called Reverend Baker and apologized for the way I'd acted and invited him over to have a look at what I'd been working on. When he saw what I was doing, he asked me to testify to the congregation about End Times Press and the tracts we'd be publishing.

The glass of water he'd given me was shaking as I walked onstage to the podium. I hadn't been able to eat anything that morning, but still felt like I might throw up. I looked at the audience, realized I didn't want to look them in the eyes, and picked up one of my tracts.

"This is . . . uh . . . my first, um, tract. It's called 'Are You Ready For,' uh, 'The Rapture,' and it . . . it's about . . . um . . ."

I took a drink of water and wiped my brow. The sweat was so thick my shirt was sticking to me. I opened the tract and started to read, stumbling over the words.

"I'm sorry. I'm not sure I can, uh . . ."

The congregation began to encourage me, "Come on, brother" and "Help him, Lord" flowed up to me from all sides. I took another drink and a deep breath, and asked the Lord to speak through me. Amens from even more people.

I told the congregation how the Lord had spoken to me one Sunday afternoon a month or so ago through a billboard. I realized what The Devil was trying to do to good Christian families, exposing children to sex and liquor at inappropriate ages, and no one was doing anything about it. How I'd quit my job so I could devote myself to my mission full-time. How I'd realized that the only way to fight fire was with fire, and I'd decided to start publishing tracts to warn people of the End Times, advertising the straight and narrow path, not the wide and wicked road. I told the congregation that I appreciated any support they could give, and asked them to keep me in their prayers.

Reverend Baker stood next to me behind the pulpit. "I've

got an announcement, brothers and sisters. The Sunday afternoon crusade two weeks from now will be devoted to distributing Brother Jody's new tracts."

There were amens and hallelujahs from around the auditorium. The preacher clapped me on the back. I finished my water and thanked them for all they'd done. Then he told the deacons to pass around the collection plates for a special offering for End Times Press.

The congregation of First Church of the Pentecost, which doesn't have a single member who makes over $30,000 a year, donated all the equipment and supplies for my first run of tracts.

The *Texarkana Gazette* had a story on the bottom of the front page about the missing beer girl around a week after she'd been at my house. The article said the brewery had found her car and when the police checked her apartment, someone had broken in. Sources said there were vague hints of gang connections.

I expected the police to show up asking about my crusade next to the billboard, so I was all prayed-up and ready when a detective knocked on my door.

"Just a few questions, Mr. Simmons, and I'll let you get back to work. Did you know Tonya Fairbanks?"

"Who?"

"The woman from the beer sign on State Line. Some of our officers said you were there passing out fliers."

"Yes sir, I passed out fliers there, but I'm moving into pamphlets now."

"So you didn't know Ms. Fairbanks? The officers said you were pretty worked up about the billboard."

"She's just a face in the ad, I never knew her name. It's the ad I'm opposed to, regardless of who's in it."

The detective wrote something down, nodded a little. His tongue poked out from between his lips as he scribbled.

"Do you happen to remember where you were ten days ago between noon and six?"

"I went to Wal-Mart to pick up some stuff, then I came home and started working on my tracts." I told him about the press and the stresses of starting a new business, even showed him some of my new tracts. He nodded and wrote, tongue sticking out.

"That's about all I have, Mr. Simmons," he said. "But here's my card if anything else comes up."

"Do you think you'll find her?"

He shrugged. "Right now it's looking like one of the local gangs might have followed her to work then broke into her home. Don't really like to think about it much after that."

After the detective left, my heart slowed again. They'd given me no reason to be nervous. He had questioned me in my living room and left a card. If they wanted to rattle my cage, they'd have brought me down to the station and asked me a lot of questions there. I'd also caught a break with someone burgling her apartment, so there was another trail for the investigators to chase. God had certainly blessed my mission.

And then, for the first time since I'd brought the Whore to the garage, I thought about the flier she'd signed.

Sweat poured down my forehead as I searched the house and car for the flier. I couldn't find it anywhere. The irrefutable evidence that she and I had actually met, and I didn't have a clue where it was.

Some Babylon employee walking across the lot, looking down. By his tire, the yellow piece of paper. He picks it up and sees the missing girl's autograph next to verses about the End Times. He stops at the police station on his way home. Men with badges on my doorstep. A courtroom expert testifying that my fingerprints are all over it next to hers.

But it didn't necessarily prove anything. Someone could have taken the flier and stuffed it in their pocket, then when they met her, looked for a piece of paper and found a flier in their pocket. It didn't *have* to be me that handed her the flier. After all, why would a Christian publisher want a beer girl's autograph?

Still, I wanted to have the bright yellow flier in my hands, so I could watch as smoke curled its corners.

The Friday before the crusade, Babylon put up a new billboard. This one had two girls: a brunette and a redhead, wearing tiny bikinis, bottles of beer nestled near cleavage. In large red letters above them was the phrase:

LIVE DELICIOUSLY

This was a problem. With the high profile of the missing first Whore of Babylon, security around these girls would be tight. The police were watching, and now so was the church. Not to mention getting to both girls at the same time was probably impossible.

I considered bombing the Babylon brewery, or hiring someone unrelated to the church to go after one of the Whores, with the hope that maybe the other would repent and ask that the sign be taken down. Some nigger maybe, to keep the cops on the gang scent.

Then I realized no matter what I did, if it wasn't part of God's Divine Plan, it wasn't going to work. He would work in His Own Way on His Own Time. I just had to wait.

How much she hath glorified herself, and lived deliciously, so much torment and sorrow give her; for she saith in her heart, I sit a queen . . . and shall see no sorrow. Therefore shall her plagues come in one day, death, and mourning, and famine; and she shall be utterly burned with fire: for strong is the Lord God who judgeth her.

— Revelations 18:7-8

For the first time in a long while, I thought about the Whore of Babylon with lust in my heart. *How soft her skin is, the wet muscular feel of her tongue in my mouth, the shape of her nipples as she lies on the floor, no longer breathing.*

I prayed for deliverance. It was slow in coming.

The new Whores of Babylon danced through my thoughts, but their images were not too ingrained yet and left easily. The blonde one, however, would not leave my mind.

I turned on my bedside lamp and opened my Bible. I tried to keep my eyes on the scriptures, but they kept drifting to the lamp. I ran a finger along my forehead, traced the barely visible line where the other lamp had cut me. Feeling the cut, I thought again of the Whore, how I'd fallen into her trap and almost lost everything. I had wanted her so badly that I didn't see she was working against me, jeopardizing my mission for God.

I didn't want to kill her, not really. I thought she would be a strong ally, someone who had been inside the world of sin and had seen the light. She had been an instrument of lust, to tempt men into drunkenness and fornication, and I'd shown her the error of her ways and brought her into church.

Except it didn't quite work out that way. She had deceived me. I had to kill her; it had been God's Will. But I was still very sad about it.

On Sunday afternoon, the sidewalks along both sides of State Line were packed with people from First Church of the Pentecost, as well as members from the nearby Fairland Holiness Church and Tabernacle of the Cross. Traffic crawled along, horns and obscenities sounding for miles. A group of women shouted at some of our members, telling them to mind their own business and stop trying to scare their children. One of the church people from Fairland told them that it was the naked girls on billboards inspiring all the violence in the world, tainting our children with the evils of lust and drunkenness by advertising such filth so openly. How else, this church member said, could you explain what had happened to the last Babylon girl?

The women began pointing fingers and cursing. Something more might have happened, but the police showed up, breaking up the argument. They also warned everyone to only pass out tracts to people who asked and to stop handing them out while drivers waited at red lights.

At the end of the day, we had passed out my entire first run of tracts. I was also invited to speak at both of the other local churches and scheduled an interview on the local gospel radio station.

On Tuesday morning I read an article about the Sunday afternoon crusade in the *Gazette*. It mentioned End Times Press and had quotes from the tracts we'd passed out. Several members from each church had been interviewed, including Reverend Baker who said this about me:

Bro. Simmons is one of our most dedicated members and has breathed new life into our mission work.

There was also a quote at the end of the article by the founder and president of Babylon Brewing Co., saying they would not be intimidated by religious lunatics, gang violence, or any other deterrents, that they had a right to do business and it's a free country and blah blah blah. Basically, he wasn't changing his sinful ways.

Which just gave me more work to do. And by printing up a new batch of tracts, I didn't have a lot of time to worry about things I couldn't control.

Like the dreams. I'd hear the doorbell ring, answer it, see her rotting corpse on my doorstep. I'd wake up drenched with sweat.

Or the blackouts. I'd find myself suddenly driving somewhere and couldn't remember leaving. Or talking to someone I didn't recall inviting into my garage. Or in bed, unable to remember if I'd just gone to bed or was waking up from a long sleep.

Or I'd catch a glimpse of yellow paper on the street and have to check it, no matter where I was going or who I was with, just to make sure it wasn't the flier with her autograph.

Or I'd think about how I should have touched her nipples when I had the chance.

Or I'd see a police car and try to casually disappear in the opposite direction.

None of which included my new church responsibilities. Now that I was a Christian publisher, everyone in the congregation wanted to get involved. There was little old Sister Martha White, who wanted to publish her book of poems about the power of Jesus's love. There was Peter Jacobson, the pockmarked teen who wanted to illustrate my tracts as very graphic comic books. There were church members who wanted to ship tracts to people they knew in churches across the country.

This was all very sudden, and for the most part kept me too busy to do much of anything but pumping out tracts. But The Lord must have been watching after me, because I was about to become His instrument again.

I was supposed to do my radio interview on the noon show, but I left early to chat with the hosts and break the ice a little. I'd had as big a breakfast as my nerves would allow and had been sipping steadily from a water bottle since leaving the house. I was thinking about all the things I had to do that day—radio show, groceries, fill a few tract orders—when I looked down to check the clock. I had over an hour and a half before I had to be anywhere. Checked the light. Turned green. Leaned over to turn up the volume and—

I was spinning across the road. My neck and left shoulder hurt, a sharp pain. My windshield was fragmented.

I realized I'd been in an accident the instant before my airbag finally opened.

I got out of my car okay. Somebody helped me sit down on the curb and was asking me questions I didn't quite understand.

Then it was like someone turned on the sound again. I could hear traffic clogged up, horns honking and sirens blaring. Someone asked me if I knew where I was and what happened.

I said I'd been driving and must have hit someone. Were they okay?

The police officer shook his head. I looked in the direction of the accident. I could see brown hair and a pretty face all bloodied up. Even in her condition, I recognized her as one of the new Whores of Babylon. God's Divine Hand had been guiding my car that morning.

"Are you okay, sir?"

"That poor woman," I said.

"Our other witnesses say she ran the red light. Talking on her cell phone."

Another police officer was looking through my car. "Hey, what's this?" I heard him say, then leaned down into the back floorboard. He stood, holding a yellow square of paper.

"That's part of my work," I said, trying not to sound too nervous. I was praying hard on the inside, hoping he didn't recognize the dead Whore's scribble.

The cop read a little of the flier. "Are you that guy I was reading about in the *Gazette* yesterday?"

I nodded. The lump in my throat made it impossible to swallow.

He looked over my shoulder at the paramedics zipping up the new dead Whore. "You folks may be on to something about them lusty ladies inspiring all kinds of violence. Whatever happened to that first billboard girl, we know it was real nasty."

I felt nauseous, on the verge of passing out.

"It's a sinful world out there," he said, handing me the flier. "Keep me in your prayers, brother."

"I most certainly will, officer. I'll be sure to thank God for all your help first chance I get."

III

The "Live Deliciously" billboard disappeared three days after the *Gazette* ran the story of the model's car crash. As did the redhead in the billboard, whom no one in Texarkana ever heard from again. The fact that I'd been involved in the accident was regarded as ironic by all, and since there were a number of witnesses who had seen her run the red light, there was no suspicion that I had done it deliberately.

Which I hadn't. It was purely an act of God's Will.

I never bragged about killing the second Whore of Babylon and when church folks asked me how I felt about it, I always got real quiet, looked down at the floor, then up to the ceiling for a minute. Afterwards, I would say, "God's Will be done."

This was always the most powerful in a congregation of about three hundred, when I'd discuss my vision and what I was trying to do with End Times Press. Because I was thrust into the spotlight so often, I was rapidly improving as a speaker. I also discovered that if I was nervous or got hung up on the words, the congregation would urge me on. They saw me as an ordinary person like themselves, and helping me get through my talk made them feel more involved. This opened a lot of hearts, and at least as many purses.

I started getting lots of business and hired a staff of people from First Church of the Pentecost to help run the press. I didn't really get a chance to think about the Whores of Babylon much anymore. When my mind wasn't on the press, it was on finding a wife.

I was nearing thirty, didn't have a girlfriend, and wasn't already married. It would only be a matter of time before the church gossip mills were churning out rumors. No good would come of this gossip, be it of adultery, or even worse, homosexuality.

Neither of which was true, but the rumors would be no less deadly.

So I went to Fairland, the largest congregation in the area, and started looking for single women. Most of the girls were already married by the time they were twenty, so I had to keep my eyes on the seventeen and eighteen year-olds.

One night I struck up a conversation with a seventeen year-old named Tricia, and I took her out for dinner. On her doorstep, we shared a quick awkward kiss.

We went out on several more dates, and I became a regular at Tricia's house, eating dinner with her parents and younger sister. They asked me about the press and kidded me about grandkids. I joked back, Tricia blushing the whole time.

Two months before she turned eighteen, I proposed.

I was taking Tricia home from dinner and when we arrived, her parents weren't home. She asked me to come in.

When we got inside, she began to kiss me. I kissed her back, knowing God wouldn't mind since she was my fiancée.

"I can't wait until we're actually married," she said. "I want you to be in me so bad."

I pushed her back from me. "Hold on, Tricia. We're not married yet."

"But you're going to be my husband. I want to have sex with you."

"I think you should repent. You shouldn't be thinking about sex until we're actually married."

She got off the couch, ran to her bedroom, crying and slamming the door. I let myself out.

That night when I was lying in bed thinking of our future together, I began to feel the flesh trying to assert itself. I prayed about it, and decided that as long as I was thinking only about Tricia and what I would do with her when she was my wife, not my fiancée, God wouldn't care if I touched myself.

Reverend Baker had become one of my biggest supporters over the last few months and was honored when I asked him to preach at our wedding.

"Oh Brother Jody, it's so good to hear you've found a wife. Maybe now you can step up and become a deacon."

I thanked him and we had a moment of prayer where the reverend blessed our union. I left his office with a hug.

God had been good to me, I thought as I was leaving. I'd quit my job on faith, and He had provided. He'd gotten me out of situations I had no idea how to escape. He provided a wife for me as a reward for doing His Good Work.

I drove home in a good mood, singing along with my friends on the gospel station. Picked up the paper I'd missed that morning, came in, took my shoes and socks off. Stretched, sat down in my favorite chair, and read the first headline:

MISSING MODEL FOUND
BURIED IN LANDFILL

I read the article, but it was sparse on details. No suspects yet, but tests were being run at a top forensics lab, and the information should reopen the investigation in the next few days.

I tossed the paper aside, got on my knees and prayed. I asked for guidance—I had done His Work, now it was His turn to be faithful and just. I needed Him to show me the way out.

The doorbell.

I invited Reverend Baker in. He said he thought he had heard prayer.

"I just read that they found the first Babylon girl," I said. "I was praying that God would help them bring the killers to justice."

"It's a terrible thing, what happened to that girl," he said.

I agreed with him, waited a few seconds, then asked him what was on his mind.

"Well, I told my wife about your engagement and she wanted me to bring something over." He opened the wooden box he was carrying and a set of silver candlesticks gleamed in the light.

"It's not real silver," he said, "but if you don't tell anyone, they'll never know. Ellie and I've had them for thirty years, but we'd like to pass it on to you and Tricia."

I thanked him and set the box over by the garage door.

"It's a difficult thing, marriage. A lifelong commitment, Jody. Are you sure you're ready?"

"I think so," I said. "I'm nervous about it."

"It's natural to be nervous. Till death do us part is a long time, and I'm sure you're also a little nervous about sex. It's okay to be reluctant. It means you're trying to make the right decision."

"I just don't know if I'm ready yet. I feel like I've still got so much work to do, and I don't know if I have time for my mission work and a family."

"Brother Jody, has God ever failed to provide for you?"

"No."

"And He will provide now, if we ask." He knelt down and reached a hand out. I took his hand.

"Father," he said, "we come before You again tonight . . ."

He prayed, but I couldn't concentrate. I was thinking about how God *had* always provided, from the beginning, and how much I would need for him to provide in the very near future. If the police linked the Whore of Babylon to me, that would be the end of the press. And what would Tricia say if she discovered her fiancé had killed the billboard girl who started his career as a publisher?

"Are you okay?"

"I'm sorry," I said. "I was just a little distracted."

He stood and moved toward the door. "I hope you feel better about things."

"I have faith that things will go well."

Reverend Baker smiled. "I'm really proud of how much you've grown over the last few months, Jody. I'll admit, I was a little disturbed when you came to me about the billboard, but since then you've become a pillar of the church and a fine man of God."

I wondered for a second if he suspected me of killing the Whore of Babylon, or if the police came after me, whether Reverend Baker would tell them what I'd said to him when I first saw the sign.

"Thank you so much, Reverend," I said. "For everything. I'm sure Tricia is going to love the candlesticks. Do you think you could help me hide them in the garage, so they'll be a surprise?"

"I'd be glad to," he said, and began to walk for the door.

When he stepped inside the garage, I brought one of the candlesticks down on his head.

He was still breathing when I took his car keys out of his pocket. I backed his car into the garage and began to load the more valuable and portable items in the backseat. I broke a few windows and emptied the petty cash out of the press's safe. I tried to make the house look as trashed as possible. By the time I opened the trunk to put him inside, he was completely still.

Interstate 30 would take me west to Dallas, and 35 would take me south to Laredo and on into Mexico. Like the prophets of the Old Testament, I too would live in the desert lands and listen for the words of my God.

Going Retro

for Michelle McKinney

*He who makes a beast of himself gets rid of
the pain of being a man.*

— Samuel Johnson

MIRANDA AND THOM WERE two bohemians living in a cow town. She: midtwenties, ex-military (chemical specialist), black, but not necessarily proud. He: early twenties, politically active (libertarian newspaper columnist), born white and Protestant but only identified with the "protest" part. Both came from poor neighborhoods and families; both took writing and literature courses at the local cow college. They dug books by William Burroughs and Langston Hughes; jazz by Count Basie and Miles Davis; films by Luis Bunuel and David Lynch. They took all the drugs they could get their hands on and drank foreign beer. They were both straight and slept together, but didn't fuck, even though everyone who knew them believed they did.

They wrote poems, stories, screenplays, nonfiction. They made photographs, paintings, movies. They lived in a house that had been a whorehouse in the days of the iron horse. They referred to themselves as hip young trendsetters on the make.

One day while smoking a blunt laced with opium, they discussed how everything cool had been done before. There was nothing left to do but go backwards, de-evolve, relive the past but in forward-moving time. They went to the tobacconist, bought pipes, flavored tobacco, and a humidor. They affected fedoras, took to walking with canes and umbrellas. Fuck the 80s, the 70s, and especially the 60s. They were *really* going retro, back to the 50s, maybe even the 40s. They would be cool like a thermometer, dropping back in time until they were doing what no one had thought to do for decades.

Soon the theater people were wearing bowlers; frat boys lounged around the student union in smoking jackets; during rush week, the fraternities each had a flapper party. Miranda and Thom were forced to go back even farther.

They decided to go beyond the 20th Century and into the mid 1800s. They used their racial differences to make those around them uncomfortable, using slurs openly against each other with raised voices, laughing hysterically over cognac afterwards. They even attended a costume party with Thom carrying a whip, leading Miranda around in chains, demanding she refer to him as "Massa Thom." Their friends giggled somewhat uncomfortably. The ones who didn't know them tried not to make eye contact.

In spite of the indifferent response they'd gotten, it was only a few days before other students were wearing powdered wigs and pantaloons around campus, putting women in stocks and openly mocking minorities, who took it all in stride, since it was done with a sense of chic irony.

Where do we go now? Thom asked. The Romans? The Greeks? The poseurs are already wearing togas. What makes you think they won't just drop back with us?

Because they're still trying to hold onto their humanity, Miranda said. The human race has advanced as far as it can anyway. Might as well drop down a rung on the evolutionary ladder.

They bought hair growth hormones and began scraping their bare hands and feet along the ground to create hard calluses. They walked around screeching and shitting everywhere, evading the police by hiding in trees. They beat their chests, terrifying local children and pets. One of the football coaches asked them to try out for the team; they tore his office to shreds, tossing his computer through a third story window, howling in victory when it exploded on someone's car.

Similar anarchic behavior began breaking out on campus soon after. Reports of people in ape masks or painted up as tigers, bears, and lizards attacking administration offices were leaked to the media. Other beast incidents began occurring in midwestern towns, in large coastal cities. Miranda and Thom read about it in the newspaper and pounded their fists on the ground.

We've got to go back even farther, Miranda said, back where no one will dare follow.

How much farther back can we get?

All the way back. Back into the water.

It was a short drive from the former whorehouse to the lake beside the interstate. The smokestack of the nuclear power plant was visible from the road. The water was three degrees warmer than the other lakes in the state, but Miranda and Thom thought this would help their transition.

We're about to become the first truly amphibious humans to walk the earth in millennia, Miranda said.

I don't think anyone can go more retro than this, said Thom.

The warm murky water slapped sleepily against their shins, their thighs, their chests. It was time to evolve.

Acknowledgments

This book would not have been possible without a great number of people. First, thanks to the journals and editors who published these pieces in their original form: Marck Beggs of *The Arkansas Literary Forum* ("The Ringing in Her Ears"), Lynn Brewer of *Cliterature* ("Closing Time," "Ringing," "The Artist and His Muse"), K. Scott Forman of *Fear Knocks* ("Custy's Used Auto"), and all the editors of *Nomadic Underground Tuber Systems [N.U.T.S.]* ("Plea Bargain"). Nate Jordon of *Monkey Puzzle* deserves special thanks for publishing "Jawbone," "Going Retro," "Inside Man," and "The Big Wheel" in their original form, as well as publishing this collection in its entirety and providing valuable editorial insight.

"Closing Time," "Ringing," and the first section of "Whore of Babylon" also appeared as the limited edition chapbook *Jezebels* from Pistolwhip Press.

Next, I would like to thank the people who contributed ideas that inspired some of the stories in this collection: Robin Marlin Knutson, Dagny McKinley, Alyssa Piccinni, Caleb Hicks, Andrew Miller, Michelle McKinney, and Michael Karl (Ritchie).

I would also like to thank the various writers who have provided editorial comments which opened many doors for me: Keith Abbott, Junior Burke, Rikki Ducornet, Brian Evenson, Andrew Geyer, Laird Hunt, Selah Saterstrom, and Andrew Wille, as well as my Arkansas Tech and Kerouac School colleagues, many of them previously mentioned.

Finally, I would like to thank my family for all their love and support, even when they didn't understand what I was doing or why: Annette Thompson, Brian Morris, Korey Morris, Don and Ruth Vaughn, and everyone else who has ever been there.

About the Author

Nicholas B. Morris was born and raised in southwest Arkansas, splitting his childhood between small towns and farms. He was educated at Arkansas Tech University and Naropa University's Jack Kerouac School of Disembodied Poetics. He lives in Denver, Colorado with his partner Alyssa Piccinni.

Other Books From
MONKEY PUZZLE PRESS

"Sexy, gutsy, raw . . . Nancy Stohlman lures us through the layers of her dark world with the promise of exposing the ultimate sparkle . . . and ends up revealing something profound."

- Raymond Federman, author of *Double or Nothing*

Fiction / $11.95
Paperback: 96 pages
Published: November 2009
ISBN-10: 0-9801650-6-7

"*The Aftermath, etc.* is a rare look at the broken man in his natural environment: a wasteland . . . his only escape is through the pen, and if it were not so, the fine art of handmade explosives."

- Andi Todaro, author of *Why My Penis Is Bigger Than Yours*

Poetry / $15.00
Paperback: 104 pages
Published: May 2010
ISBN-10: 0-9826646-2-1

"Surprises here for everyone who loves and studies art: 'particular things/ Begin to mouse-rush in the domestic box./ So thought's a gardener, crazy like a fox.'"

- Reed Bye, author of *Join the Planets*

Poetry / $16.00
Paperback: 96 pages
Published: May 2010
ISBN-10: 0-9826646-0-5